THE ZOMBIE CHASERS
WORLD ZOMBINATION

BY JOHN KLOEPFER

ILLUSTRATED BY
DAVID DeGRAND

HARPER

An Imprint of HarperCollinsPublishers

Library of Congress Control Number: 2015943577
ISBN 978-0-06-229027-4 (trade bdg.)

15 16 17 18 19   CG/RRDH   10 9 8 7 6 5 4 3 2 1
❖
First Edition

To my sweet Jenny Lee from sunny Tennessee

—J. K.

For Dana and Hagen

—D. D.

CHAPTER

The rain forest buzzed and hummed like it was alive.

Zack Clarke led the way through the damp Madagascar jungle, and his older sister, Zoe, followed close behind. His friends Rice, Ozzie, and Madison trailed along with Madison's Canadian cousin, Olivia Jenkins, safe between them. Olivia was the key to unzombifying the undead masses—because of her strict vegan diet and obsession with Vital Vegan PowerPunch, her favorite flavor of the ginkgo biloba–infused vitamin water. Madison's dog, Twinkles, trotted next to them, always on the lookout. The group had to make sure

Olivia didn't get ripped apart by a zombie, or all hope for the cure would be lost.

Their feet squished in the moss-covered ground as they pushed deeper into the rain forest. A high-pitched squawk chattered from above. Zack glanced up as two ring-tailed lemurs swung from branch to branch, then disappeared into the treetops. He wasn't a big fan of the

jungle. There were too many creepy noises: loud, wild cackles and unfamiliar hoots. A zombie could be lurking behind every corner. Or even worse, some kind of deadly zombie wildlife.

Zack hoped that their journey would be over soon and they'd be able to head back to Nigel Black's lab to mix up the antidote.

Nigel Black was their newfound friend and zombie expert, who had an amazing lab on his private island fortress in the Caribbean. He was an aging ex-explorer who once had his own television show: *Nigel Black's Unnatural Wonders*. Just like Zack, Nigel wanted to rid the world of zombies, but only if he didn't have to leave his island.

Now Zack and his friends were some of the only humans left in the world. And they were definitely the only ones with the know-how to stop the outbreak once and for all.

Zack thought back over the last day and a half, when they had speared the giant frilled tiger shark and brought it back to Nigel—it already seemed like so long ago. The digestive enzyme of the giant frilled tiger shark was supposed to produce a cure that would reverse the mutated zombie virus.

However, after they added the enzyme to the serum, the super zombie antidote still hadn't worked. Nigel then ran a few tests and had figured out that they needed "one more" ingredient: a special type of African mayfly larvae found only in Madagascar. And so Olivia's brother, Ben, remained super-zombified back at Nigel Black's lab.

Rice had a sample of the giant frilled tiger shark enzyme in his backpack, along with an empty container in which to bring back the mayfly larvae to Nigel.

That's how they'd ended up here, tromping through Madagascar. It was the final stop on their journey to find the last ingredient for the super zombie antidote.

There was nothing they could do until they returned with the sample.

That is, *if* they returned.

The group had landed in the jungle less than an hour ago and left their plane safely parked on the coast.

Now as Zack trekked through the thick, leafy underbrush with his friends, his sister's voice startled him and he froze.

"Yo, little bro," Zoe said suddenly in a fearful voice. "Don't move. . . ."

"What?" Zack looked back over his shoulder at his sister. "Why?"

"Because . . ." Zoe's eyes bugged out as she pointed at the top of Zack's head. The rest of the gang came to a halt behind her. "There's a tarantula crawling up your shoulder!"

The mere mention of the word *tarantula* made Zack's heart skip a beat. He was a huge arachnophobe. He hated spiders so much he couldn't help but shudder at the sight of a harmless daddy longlegs.

"OMG, it's a big one!" Zoe shouted.

"Wha—" Zack freaked out and smacked his head over and over, trying to knock the furry-legged spider off him. "Eek-eek!"

"Arf! Arf!" Twinkles barked in response, prancing on his tiny legs.

A burst of laughter erupted from the girls. Zoe, Madison, and Olivia doubled over, giggling like a bunch of maniacs.

"What's so funny?" Zack cried, slapping himself and wriggling in place like he was doing some kind of weird hip-hop dance. "Get it off me!"

"There's nothing on your head, dude," Rice told

his best friend. Rice loved pulling pranks, but even he knew
when they needed to get
serious. At least most of
the time he did. "She's
just messing with you."

Zack stopped his freak-
out dance and glared at his
big sis, his blood boiling. "Why
would you do that?" he asked, knowing
he wasn't going to get a good answer.

"Cuz it was hilarious!" She was still bent over with
laughter.

"Enough joking around," Ozzie said. "We all need
to stay focused." Ozzie was good at taking charge and
reminding the group that they had a mission. Zack
appreciated that his friend kept them on track.

"Yes, sir, Ozzie, sir!" Zoe straightened up and
saluted him.

Ozzie shook his head at her and kept walking.

As they headed inland toward the river, Zack couldn't

shake the feeling that someone or something was watching them.

They were following Nigel Black's map and directions, which told them that the larvae would be along the riverbank, but Zack still had absolutely no idea where exactly. He hoped that someone did.

"Okay, show me the map. Let's get the sample and get out of here," Madison said. "This whole place could be zombified for all we know."

"Quit being so paranoid," Olivia weighed in. "We're on an island. Not a lot of tourists. I think we're out of harm's way for a while."

Zack and Ozzie each shot their buddy a look.

"What?" said Olivia, flipping up the palms of her hands.

"Thanks for jinxing us!" Ozzie and Zack said at the exact same time.

"Hah!" Olivia pointed at them. "You just jinxed yourselves."

Suddenly Zack heard a rustle in the underbrush and turned his head. "What was that?" He scanned the dark green thicket of the rain forest.

"What was what?" Ozzie asked, lowering his voice to a whisper.

A dozen yellow eyes flashed out of the shadowy spaces between the trees.

"That . . ." Zack pointed to their right.

A pack of six ring-tailed lemurs stalked out of the rain forest, frothing at the mouth, all gibbering like a tunnel full of crazed sewer rats.

Ozzie snapped into fight mode and whirled his nunchaku at the zombified monkeys. "Zack, Zoe, you guys distract them from the right," Ozzie ordered. "Rice, Madison, you two flank from the left. I'll go in straight on."

"What do I do?" Olivia asked.

"You hang back," Ozzie said.

"Why do I always have to hang back?"

"Because we have to protect you," Rice said. "You're the antidote."

Olivia rolled her eyes. "Just because I'm a vegan and my blood unzombifies people doesn't make me some damsel in distress. I can stick up for myself. . . ."

"They used to do the same thing when I was the antidote," Madison said, getting into position. "It was super annoying. But it did save my butt a few times."

"Okay, guys," Zoe said, edging away from the zombified lemurs moving toward them. "Can we just get the heck out of here, please?"

"Heads up!" Ozzie shouted as one of the lemurs

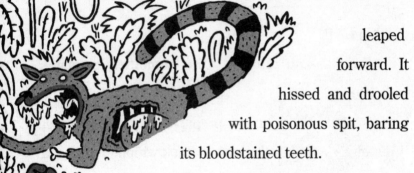

leaped forward. It hissed and drooled with poisonous spit, baring its bloodstained teeth.

Without hesitating, Ozzie spun around and whipped his arm out like he was snapping a shower towel after gym class. The nunchaku's chain shot out and clocked the undead lemur, knocking it to the ground.

"Arf-arf-arf!" Twinkles charged at the zombie critters as they closed in. The lemurs paused, not knowing what to make of the ferocious little mutt.

"Twinkles, get back here," Madison commanded, but the tiny pup barked and snarled. "Twinkles!"

The lemurs crept forward. Their black-and-white ringed tails arched over their heads like scorpions with their stingers about to thrust and stab with poison.

"Arf-arf!"

"Kah-kah-kah-kah-kah!" the zombified primates jabbered.

As the undead lemurs prepared to pounce, something else rustled in the leaves. Zack whipped his head around toward the noise.

Tweeeeeeeeeeeeeeeeet! A high-pitched whistle sounded from the depths of the jungle, and the zombie lemurs froze in place. They put their grubby little paws over their ears, clutching their heads. *Tweeeeeeeet!*

Out of the dark foliage, a lone figure emerged.

Tweeeet! the noise came again. Zack recoiled in fear, wondering what this new danger could be.

CHAPTER

The figure strode out of the shadows, coming straight toward them. Its hands curled up toward its mouth, which looked like it was full of wooden teeth. Its eyeballs bulged.

Zack squinted, trying to focus on the zombie and assess the threat. Then he realized that this zombie wasn't a zombie at all but a young girl of about thirteen, holding a flute to her lips.

The piercing note sounded again, and the undead lemurs ran back into the rain forest.

"Could you please not hit the lemurs with your nunchaku?" the girl asked, looking at Ozzie.

"What was I supposed to do?" Ozzie said defensively. "That thing was going to rip my eyes out and eat my brains out of the sockets!"

"He's right," Rice said. "Those lemurs had it in for us."

"I know," she said. "Zombie lemurs are a big problem here right now, but lemurs are an endangered species. So next time, use this. . . ." The girl tossed her whistle to Zack. He caught it and turned it over in his hand. He saw that it was a square wooden flute made out of reeds, like a panpipe.

"What is it?" Zack asked.

"Made it myself," the girl said. "It plays at a frequency these undead animals can't stand. Discovered it by accident. It works on lemurs, most birds, even fossa."

"What's a fossa?" Madison asked.

"They're, like, these really cute cougar things," the girl said. "But they're kind of vicious. Even when they're not zombified."

"And how do you know so much?" Zoe asked. "Who are you?"

"Oh sorry." The girl reached out to shake Zoe's hand. "I'm Nadie."

"I'm Zoe," she said, then pointed at her friends. "And this is my BFF, Madison, and that's her cousin, Olivia. And those little nerd bombers over there are my brother, Zack; his friend Rice; and Ozzie."

"So what brings you guys here to Madagascar?" Nadie asked.

"It's a long story," Rice said. "But we're trying to find the super zombie antidote to unzombify everyone."

"And stop the super zombies," Olivia chimed in. "We already have the regular zombie antidote. That would be me."

"But right now, we need to get to the mayfly larvae," Zack added.

Nadie shot them a confused look. "What's a super zombie?"

"We made them by accident," Zack explained, "because we wanted to make a permanent antidote. Rice sorta dropped the ball on that one."

"Hey!" Rice said defensively.

"What?" said Zack. "You did."

"Yeah, now there are all these weirdo freakazoid zombies running around, thinking they're smarter than us," Zoe said. "And they want to kidnap Olivia so they can unzombify the regular zombies and feast on their brains."

"Are you serious?" Nadie's eyeballs bugged out of her face. "That sounds like a totally unsustainable ecosystem."

"Totes," said Madison, pointing at Nadie. "What she said."

"Huh? What's *totes*?" Nadie asked, looking confused. "You mean like a tote bag?"

"No, like totes . . . ," said Madison. "Totes magotes? Totally."

"Oh . . ." Nadie's voice trailed off.

"You'll have to excuse them," Rice jumped in. "They're speaking Moronese."

"Yeah," Zack said. "It's kind of like English, only way stupider."

"It's better than speaking Dorklish," Zoe snipped, and then turned to Nadie. "That's their preferred language."

"I have no idea what you guys are talking about," Nadie said. "But we should probably get out of here. The jungle's not safe. Even with the zombie whistle."

"But wait a minute." Ozzie stopped them. "We have to get the mayfly sample first, remember?"

"Why do you need mayfly larvae anyway?" Nadie asked, scrunching up her face. "I don't get how that's a cure."

"By itself, it's not. We need to mix the larvae with the giant frilled tiger shark enzyme so it can counteract the super zombie virus mutation by shortening its lifespan and dissolving the Caribbean sea plankton from the Spazola Energy Cola that caused the super zombie virus in the first place . . . ," Zack said quickly before running out of breath.

"Oh," Nadie said, considering Zack's explanation thoughtfully. "That makes sense."

Madison furrowed her eyebrows. "It does?"

"Sure, but you're not going to find any mayflies around here," Nadie said. "They're way upstream. I can give you a ride if you want."

"That would be totes amaze—!" Zoe said, then corrected herself. "I mean, that would be totally amazing!"

"Riiiight," Nadie said. "But we should hurry. The mayfly's mating season is half over and their larvae are about to hatch. So if you're trying to get a sample, it's

now or wait another six months. . . ."

Six months? There's no way we can wait that long, Zack thought. If they didn't get the mayfly sample back to Nigel as soon as possible, there wouldn't be anything left for them to save. By then the world might be totally overrun by Uncle Conrad, Aunt Ginny, Cousin Ben's pirate hordes, and the rest of the super zombies.

"We have to hurry," Zack said. The jungle was full of undead danger, and the clock was ticking.

Nadie led them back through the gloomy rain forest until they reached her Jeep. They all piled in as Nadie revved the engine. They raced out of the jungle and onto a narrow dirt road that wove through the grassy plains of Madagascar.

"What are you doing in Madagascar?" Ozzie asked Nadie as they drove along.

"Well, my parents are wildlife conservationists and they're stationed here, so . . . that kind of means I'm stationed here, too. It's pretty awesome actually. There are all types of cool animals here and I'm allowed to drive. Well, it used to be awesome before everything got zombified, anyway."

As they cruised across the flatlands, a slew of baobab trees stood tall, raising their tangled limbs to the dark clouds overhead.

"Looks like we're going to get a free shower," Nadie said, glancing up at the sky.

"Awesome," Zoe said, pinching her nose. "No offense, Zack, but you're really starting to stink."

Zack lifted his arm and sniffed his armpit. "Am not!"

"Are, too!"

"So, Nadie, where are your parents?" Rice asked while Zack and Zoe continued their debate over who smelled the worst. "You can't be the only person on the island."

"Well," she said. "I might be the only non-zombie person. I haven't run into any locals yet who are still human. My parents rezombified and started going berserk. Before anyone knew what was happening, they had bitten a few people and then *they* zombified and bit a few people and then our whole village was totes zombified except for me. Did I use that right?"

"Totes." Madison nodded and gave her a wink.

"I corralled everyone I could into the rehabilitation facility and locked it. The rest are quarantined in the pen where we usually keep the sick animals. So they're safe, for now. Ever since they all zombified or rezombified or whatever, I've taken over as wildlife conservationist."

"Wow," Olivia said. "It's amazing you haven't been bitten yet."

"I've had a few close calls. My trusty whistle got me out of a few scrapes with the fossa," Nadie said. "But no bites yet." She crossed her fingers and smiled.

"But wait a minute," Ozzie said. "How did your parents rezombify if you live in Madagascar? The first outbreak was only in America."

"We've only been here for about six months," she told them. "Before that, we lived in Michigan. I was lucky enough to survive the entire outbreak, but my parents weren't so fortunate. We hadn't eaten anything in days. We came across an abandoned rest stop on the side of the highway. BurgerDog was one of the restaurants. We didn't know that that's what was turning people into zombies. I didn't eat the burger patties. I had chips instead, but they ate the burgers and turned into zombies right then and there. I ran away from them, but soon after, I heard planes zooming overhead and all of a sudden all this pink popcorn rained down from the sky and unzombified everything. It was a miracle."

A proud smirk curled up at the corner of Ozzie's mouth. "Yeah, that was us," he said.

"We're kind of miraculous," added Rice.

"Wait minute," Nadie said. "You're the Zombie Chasers?"

"In the flesh!" said Zack.

"Cool!" Nadie said. "Now I get why you guys are here." She turned down another dusty dirt road.

"Hey, Nadie!" Ozzie called from the back of the Jeep. "Might want to see if this thing can go any faster."

"Why?" Nadie asked, checking the rearview mirror.

In the backseat, Ozzie pressed his binoculars to his face and looked behind them. Two zombified ostriches were chasing after them in hot pursuit of their Jeep. Croaking and flapping their big-feathered wings, their long necks bobbed and green patches of diseased skin spread from under their beaks and up the sides of their heads.

"They're gaining on us!" Ozzie shouted over the growl of the car as Nadie tried to rev the engine.

Without looking away from the steering wheel, Nadie called back. "I can't go any faster!"

The zombified ostriches were right at their backs, clacking their beaks and trying to snap at the wheels.

"Try the whistle!" Zoe shouted.

Quickly, Zack pulled out the antizombie whistle and blew. *Tweeeet!* the whistle piped, but the birds were unfazed by the sound.

"It's not working!" Zack yelled, and Ozzie took out his nunchaku.

"Sorry, Nadie," he said. "Sometimes you gotta do what you gotta do." With a deft flick of his wrist, Ozzie

struck the ostrich on his left. *THWAP!*

The wooden handle socked the zombie bird in the side of its skull, and the ostrich tripped and flopped to the ground. The Jeep sped on, leaving the foul fowl in the dust.

On the other side of the Jeep, the second zombie ostrich snapped at Madison and Zoe, its sharp beak nearly pecking out their eyeballs.

Zoe shrieked, "It's got me! Help!"

The bird's giant beak nipped her by the sleeve and yanked her over the side. *"OOF!"*

Madison's reflexes kicked in, and she clutched Zoe's leg with both hands. "Guys, help!" Madison cried, holding on to her BFF as hard as she could.

Olivia grabbed one of Zoe's ankles and hung on tight.

"You guys, it's going to eat me!" Zoe screamed over the loud phlegmy grunts of the ostrich. "Don't let go!"

If they didn't pull Zoe back in, the ostrich was going to peck her to death and rip her limb from limb.

"Pull her up!" Zack shouted from the front seat, and started to climb toward the back to help.

"We're trying!" Madison shouted.

"I can't hold on!" Madison yelled as Zoe's leg slipped from her grasp.

Olivia jerked to the side and nearly tumbled over the side of the Jeep, too. Her fingers were hooked in the laces of Zoe's shoe, the only thing between Zoe living and undying. But her laces were slowing coming undone as the ostrich tugged harder.

In a flash Ozzie scrambled across the backseat and brought his nunchaku off his hip. He threw one end out toward Zoe, and she grabbed it with her free hand. Olivia's fingers went from red to purple right before Zoe's shoelaces slipped from her grasp. Ozzie pulled back on the other end of the nunchaku and Zack prayed Ozzie's weapon wouldn't snap in half.

SCKRYYCK! Zoe's shirtsleeve ripped off in the ostrich's beak, and the zombified bird swerved away for a second with the piece of fabric in its mouth. The ostrich ogled the kids as it ran, gobbling the ripped-off sleeve down its gullet in one long gulp. Zoe's body flopped over the side of the Jeep, her hair dangling just inches from the ground. Everything sped by at forty miles an hour. She did a vertical sit-up against the outer side of the speeding Jeep, and with one massive grunt, the whole group helped pull her up to safety. She landed back in her seat with a thud and breathed a sigh of relief. The ostrich lashed out once more, but Ozzie knocked it out cold, cracking the big undead bird on the noggin.

"Nice shot, Oz!" Zoe shouted, and pumped her fist in the air.

The zombified ostrich tumbled into a cloud of dirt and the Jeep sped out of danger. As they drove on, the daylight darkened to twilight, and a loud thunderclap banged nearby. Storm clouds blotted out the sun, and the sky opened up. Zack felt the downpour all at once, a thousand drops soaking him to the bone in less than an instant. It was so hot that the rain actually felt good, but the wind picked up, dropping their visibility to zero. The flatlands became a giant muddy muddle.

"We have to take a detour into the jungle," Nadie said, squinting through the water. "The rain won't be as bad." Mud splashed up the sides of the Jeep as she steered off the road and through the trees.

This was going to be a bumpy ride.

CHAPTER 3

The wind and rain calmed down once they drove under the cover of the trees. They plowed through deep tracks of mud, and Zack hoped they wouldn't get stuck. Rainwater poured off the canopy of leaves like a thousand water faucets on full blast.

The terrain was filling up with runoff from the downpour, and they soon found themselves plunging through half a foot of mud, which was rising by the second.

"We have to get to higher ground!" Ozzie shouted over the sound of the storm. "Don't want to flood the engine!"

Nadie nodded and spun the wheel. They veered up

a steep incline to get above the flash flood. As Nadie straightened out the Jeep, a demonic hiss sounded above them. Another zombified lemur dropped down, landing on Nadie's shoulder. Its ringed tail was gone, and all of its fur had fallen off, leaving nothing but a wiggling piece of decomposing skin and bone.

The lemur reared its head back to chomp down on her neck. Nadie shrieked and the vehicle swerved. In the passenger's seat, Zack sucked in and blew into the whistle at the last second. *Tweeeeeeeeet!*

The undead lemur flinched at the noise and Olivia reached up from the backseat, grabbed the brain-craving critter, and hurled it away from the Jeep.

"Omigosh!" Nadie gripped the steering wheel tightly, but they were spinning out of control. The Jeep tipped forward and slid down a hill and Nadie slammed the brakes. They all jerked to a stop. "Sorry, that thing just scared the heck out of me!"

"You okay?" Zack asked, looking at Nadie's neck for any wounds. She was free of any bite marks but seemed a little rattled.

"I think so . . . ," she said. "Thanks for saving me, Zack."

"No problem," he said.

"I'm glad everyone's okay, but can we please get out of this place?" Madison said.

"You got it!" Nadie pushed the accelerator down with her foot and the engine revved.

But the Jeep didn't move.

Zack peered over the side. The tires were stuck deep in a foot and a half of mud. Nadie revved the engine again. The rear wheels spun and sprayed twin arcs of brown muck up into the air.

Zack had a bad feeling. He wanted to get out of the rain forest as soon as they could. The reek of undead bush meat, mixed with the thick humidity, made him want to vomit.

Nadie jammed the accelerator again with her foot, but the Jeep wouldn't budge. "Looks like we're going to have to get out and push," she told them.

"All right, let's do this, guys." Zoe was the first to jump out, not caring if she got dirty as long as they got out of there.

They all followed her lead and leaped out of the Jeep and landed up to their knees in the deep, jungle muck. But as soon as they were out of the safety of their vehicle, zombified animals began attacking from all sides. More monkeys gibbered and jabbered high in the tree branches. Birds flapped wildly above their heads.

"EEEK!" Zoe shrieked as a green and orange tropical bird planted its talons in her hair. She grabbed the zombified bird off her head. *WHAM!* Zoe flung the bird away and it bonked against a tree and slid down the trunk.

Quickly, Zack and his friends sloshed through the water to the back of the vehicle. Nadie put the gearshift in neutral and the six of them gave the back bumper a push.

Nothing. The front tires had sunk too deep in the mud.

Over the sound of the pouring rain, Zack thought he could hear something else coming from the jungle. It was the low moans of despair and yearning for human brains. As he scanned the tree line, thunder and

lightning boomed, illuminating four human zombies emerging from the forest.

The grim-faced ghouls had blotches of fungus growing on their cheeks and foreheads. Their teeth were sharp and chiseled to little points from gnawing on bones.

"Glargh!" the four mutants gargled as they staggered toward the seven Zombie Chasers.

"Arf! Arf!" Twinkles yapped nonstop, barking his head off.

The zombies gawped at the kids, bug-eyed, snapping their jaws, clacking their razor-sharp teeth. Zack

didn't like the look of them. They seemed a bit quicker than regular, tubby American zombies. The undead islanders stumbled nimbly through the mud, lashing out with their fingernails, squawking and snarling.

"I thought you said everyone was in the facility!" Zack said.

"Everyone from my village," said Nadie from inside the Jeep. "Not everyone on the whole island."

"Well, that would have been helpful information," Rice said.

"We need to get out of here," Nadie said. "If there's four of them, that means there could be four hundred right behind them."

"This isn't working!" Madison cried, still trying to push the Jeep along with Zoe, Ozzie, and Olivia.

"Looks like we're going to have to escape on foot," Nadie said. "There's a boat on the riverbank not too far from here. . . . Let's go!" She hopped out of the driver's

seat and started to lead them deeper into the jungle, away from the zombies.

"Hold on a minute," Zack said. "The whistle!" He spun on his heel and doubled back for the Jeep.

"Zack, come on!" Madison shouted. "There's no time. Those things are getting close!"

But Zack didn't listen. He took off, sloshing through the flood, as the undead natives shambled out of the trees. There must have been more than two dozen of them now, staggering forward along with the insane zombie wildlife.

Zack could see Nadie's whistle on the passenger seat, right where he'd left it. He stretched his arm across the front seat and snatched it up. The flood was past his knees now and Zack thought he felt something scurry around his calf muscle underwater. He felt the whistle in his hand when Ozzie's voice rang out behind him.

"Zack, look out!" Ozzie shouted.

"Snake!"

"Huh?" Zack swiveled his head from side to side, but all he saw were the zombified locals headed toward the Jeep. He looked back at Ozzie. "Not funny, man!"

"For real, man!" Ozzie shouted, pointing at something above Zack's head.

Zack glanced straight above him and—ZSSSSSSSSSS—a giant snake hissed and dropped down from a tree branch overhead.

"AHHHH!" Zack shrieked as the zombified snake coiled around his arm and squeezed. It felt like when the doctor checked his blood pressure. The boa constrictor was twice as thick as Zack's arm and four times as strong. He had to act quickly if he wanted to keep his arm, which he most certainly did. He really liked his arm, especially when it was attached to the rest of his body. The only problem was that the antizombie whistle was now in the clutches of the constrictor. Before the snake could coil around again and squeeze even tighter, Zack flipped the whistle in the air and caught it with his other hand. He blew into it, like a harmonica, but the boa wasn't even affected by the high-pitched tweet.

Zack tugged his arm back, but the zombie snake's grip tightened. It stretched its jaws above Zack's hand and Zack tugged with all his might. Just as the snake lashed out to sink its fangs into him, Zack's arm slipped through the serpent's coiled body. The snake's open jaws barely missed Zack's hand and took a huge chomp out of its own tail instead.

Zack tucked the whistle under his arm and hustled back to his friends. Without looking back, they all took off into the jungle.

As they hiked through the mud, the rain died down to a sprinkle. They moved slowly, tracking footprints into the moist dirt, and soon Zack could see the river flowing up ahead.

As they made their way toward the riverbank, Nadie stopped abruptly and put her arms out to halt the rest of the group. "Whoa," she said as a pack of undead devil dogs skulked out of the underbrush and formed a semi-circle in front of them.

"What the heck are those things?" Zoe asked.

"Awww," Madison cooed. "They're kinda cute. . . ."

Twinkles growled, not liking them one bit. He hated any competition, and always had to be the cutest.

Nadie turned around, saw the pack of wild animals, and gasped, "Fossa!"

The zombified animals looked like a cross between a

cougar and a hyena. The pack trod closer, their mouths peeled back to show their razor-sharp fangs.

"Good thing we got that whistle back," Nadie said. "Play us a tune, Zack, will ya?"

"I don't really know any songs," he said.

"Just blow the darn thing!" Zoe yelled at her brother.

Zack raised the panpipe to his lips and blew. The fossa's ears flattened back at the sound of the tweet and they hissed, scurrying away back into the jungle bracken.

"This thing is awesome," Zack said, amazed at the antizombie whistle.

"Come on, let's get out of here," Ozzie said. "This place is swarming."

Nadie guided them to the riverbank, where they spotted a long canoe tipped over on its side, resting on the shore. "See, here it is. My dad used to use this boat for some of his expeditions."

"Everybody in!" Zack said and hurried to flip it over.

The seven of them dragged

the boat into the water. They hopped in and paddled upstream. About a half mile upriver, Nadie guided the boat toward the right-hand bank. "Here we are. This is where the mayfly larvae hatch," she said. "Just a short bit more up that way."

Out of the corner of his eye, Zack thought that rippling water seemed to be following them. The surface glugged with a few bubbles and then went still as the water settled. Zack squinted, trying to see below the surface, and then something huge lurched out of the murky river with a great splash.

"Growwrgh!" A crocodile head reared out of the river with a vicious cackle and snap.

The group quickly paddled to shore and sprang out of the boat, but the crocodile was right on their heels.

CHAPTER 4

The crocodile jumped out of the dark water with a mighty splash. It looked like it was smiling, happy to have just found its next meal. All seven of them ran back, keeping their distance. Twinkles scurried away and hid behind Madison's leg, whimpering, as the gigantic reptile scuttled up onto the riverbank. It stretched open its V-shaped snout and let out a vicious hiss.

"Whoa, cool!" Rice announced. "An alligator!"

"That's no alligator," Nadie corrected him. "That's a *Crocodylus niloticus*. . . ."

"A what-a-dillus?" Zoe asked, backing away from the beast.

"A crocodile," Nadie said. "Doesn't appear to be zombified, but that doesn't mean anything. These guys are very aggressive."

"He's a big guy, ain't he?" Olivia said, keeping her distance.

"Pretty big," Nadie agreed. "But I've seen bigger."

Bigger than that thing? Zack thought. The crocodile must have been at least eight feet long from the tip of its nose to the end of its tail.

"Come on, I'm going to need help wrangling this sucker. Too big to do alone," Nadie said, pulling out a coil of rope from her utility belt and pointing at Zack and Rice. "You two get behind him and grab him by the tail."

"Are you crazy?" Zoe said. "Zack, don't go near that thing!"

"If you want the mayfly larvae, their breeding grounds are right over there." Nadie pointed up the riverbank, past the crocodile. "These guys are very territorial. If we're going to collect a sample, we have to tie him up. Now come on, grab him by the tail. . . ."

"Excuse me, little miss crocodile hunter girl." Zoe put her hands on her hips and cocked an eyebrow at Nadie. "But I'm not about to stand here and watch my little brother get eaten by an alligator."

"Chill out, Zoe. It's not even zombified," said Rice, pushing up his sleeves. "And besides, it's a crocodile."

Zack swallowed a big, fearful gulp. "Yeah, Zoe, take a chill pill."

"Fine," she said. "Suit yourself, but don't blame me if your arm gets bitten off."

"Here, here." Nadie waved a stick in front of the crocodile's face, distracting it. "Over here, you big old nasty thing. . . ."

"Come on," Rice whispered, and Zack followed his buddy as he edged behind it. They waded into the water, doing their best to sneak up on the beast. Zack and

Rice positioned themselves behind the reptile, which snapped its powerful jaws as Nadie waved the stick back and forth. The two boys stood on either side of the crocodile's tail, their backs to the river.

"Okay now, you two are going to grab it and drag it backward up the shoreline," Nadie instructed them as fast and as calmly as she could, dodging the crocodile's clacking, razor-sharp snout.

"Are you sure you know what you're doing?" Madison asked.

Ozzie looked a little skeptical, too. "Yeah, have you done this before?"

"Not personally," Nadie said. "But I've seen my dad do it, like, a dozen times. All I have to do is jump on its back and clamp its mouth shut while one of you ties this rope around the snout."

"One of us?" Zoe asked. "Now I know you're crazy."

"Their bite is really powerful, but their jaw muscles are weak, so once you have their mouth shut, they can't open back up again," she explained, giving them a crash course on crocodiles.

"I'll do it," Olivia said, stepping forward.

"No way, too dangerous. We can't afford losing you. You're too valuable as the antidote," Ozzie said, taking the rope from Nadie. "I'll handle it."

SNAP! The crocodile's snout closed shut with a crack and the stick in Nadie's hand snapped in half.

"Yikes!" Nadie flinched back.

"Can we get on with this?" Rice asked. "Wrestling a live crocodile is on my bucket list and I'm not getting any younger."

"Don't be nervous, guys," Nadie coached him from the shore. "They can sense your fear."

"Too late," Zack said. "I'm already pretty freakin' nervous."

"Now!" Rice yelled.

The big lizard twitched as the boys each grabbed the nubby tail with both hands.

The massive reptile wriggled, but the boys held on, pulling with all their might. Just as they gained traction and began to drag the beast up onto the sand, something surged out of the water behind them: an enormous *zombified* crocodile, twice the size of the first one. It lifted its brown head and roared.

With a shriek, Zack landed butt first in the water and watched as the zombie chomped down and bit the other crocodile's tail in half.

The smaller, soon-to-be-zombified crocodile made a strange sound, almost like a whimpering yelp. It lumbered away from the river with a waddle, past the kids, and left a thick trail of blood behind it as it escaped into the jungle.

"GLRGHOWRK!" The undead crocodile glugged down the tail and let out a revolting burp, then whipped its head at Zack and Rice. Its eyeballs were bright red

and bloodshot, oozing some kind of nasty yellow pus. A huge bite mark had left its hindquarters mangled on the left side. But that didn't stop the massive zombie from lunging at Zack and Rice, who were crab-walking into the river to get away from the monster.

Zack splashed and flailed as the crocodile snapped at him. He stared straight down its throat, so close that he could smell the rancid stink of other half-digested animals. Rice squealed in fear. They were trapped—if they went any deeper into the river, they'd have to start swimming. And Zack didn't want to think about what else was in the water.

Nadie sprang into action, grabbing the zombie croc by the tail. "Hurry! Drag it back onto land. If it gets them in the water, they're both goners!" Nadie, Madison, Zoe, and Olivia clung to the crocodile's tail,

digging their feet into the sand and playing tug-of-war against the animal's desire to make a snack out of Zack's and Rice's brains.

But as the girls heaved and hoed, the crocodile slid backward. Zack and Rice watched as Ozzie leaped onto the beast and mounted its back.

The zombie crocodile lurched violently, trying to buck Ozzie off its spine, but he rode the giant lizard like a champion cowboy at the rodeo. He grappled his way up to the crocodile's neck and lashed Nadie's rope around its muzzle, knotting it tightly so the zombie croc could no longer open its mouth.

The crocodile thrashed as Rice and Zack ran back onto solid ground. It took all seven of them to flip the zombie croc on its back, but as soon as they did, the beast was harmless and the riverbank upstream was free and clear.

"You did it!" Zack gave Ozzie a high five.

They all followed Nadie up the riverbank and slowed down as their guide came to a stop.

"There they are!" Nadie pointed to a muddy spot

at the edge of the jungle river.

The mayfly larvae covered the top of the wet soil, a squirming translucent film of bug eggs.

"Ew, gross!" Madison squelched her face in disgust. "So nasty."

"Not as nasty as a bunch of super zombies," said Zoe. "No offense to your family, Olivia."

"None taken," Olivia said as Rice pulled out the special container from Nigel.

"And now it's time to make history," he said. "Zombie history."

"The only one who's going to make zombies history is me!" said Zoe as she snatched the container from Rice.

"Hey!" Rice shouted, but she ignored him and stepped toward the mayflies.

"Come on, let's go!" Zack shouted to his sister as she slowly and carefully gathered the sample. "Hurry up!"

"I'm going as fast as I can," Zoe shouted back, sealing the lid. "Got it!"

"Yeah, Zo!" Madison cheered. "You go, girl . . . you go!"

Running back to the group, Zoe suddenly stumbled forward as her foot snagged a rock. She tripped face-first into a log.

Zack gasped as the larvae container flew in the air, arcing through the drizzling rain, and plopped into the river.

The container bobbed downstream, away from them.

"Zoe!" Rice shouted. "What'd you do?"

"Don't yell at me, you little lamewad. It's not like I meant to fall down," Zoe yelled. "I'm not an Olympic athlete!"

"You guys, we can't lose those mayflies," Madison said. "You heard what Nadie said! It's not going to be their mating season for another six months!"

"Why don't you just take another sample?" Nadie asked them.

"Because we need that special container to preserve them," Ozzie explained.

Zack turned to his sister. "Zoe, go get it," he yelled. "You're the one who dropped it."

"No way, José. There could be crocodiles in there," she snipped. "Why don't you go get it? You're the one who was rushing me to—"

Before Zoe could finish her sentence, Olivia had already taken off like a shot, running toward the river.

"Olivia!" Madison shouted to her cousin. "Wait . . . come back!"

But it was too late.

Zack and the gang looked on as the last of the vital

vegans dove in the water. Olivia kicked her feet, swimming after the container.

"Look," Rice shouted. "She's gaining on it!"

Olivia was gliding toward the floating sample. Zack watched as her arm reached out and snatched it out of the current.

Gracefully, she changed course and swam back to the shore. Olivia stood on the riverbank and lifted the container victoriously above her head. "All-city swim meet, first place," she bragged. "Set a record for my age bracket . . ."

"Olivia, watch out!" Zack shouted, and Olivia whirled around to find herself face-to-face with the recently zombified, tail-less crocodile waddling out of the underbrush.

The crocodile snapped its jaw with a sound like a carrot cracking in half, nearly nipping Olivia in the back of the leg. But she hopped out of the way just in time. With a squeal, she spun on her heel and ran back to her friends.

"Nice job, Olivia!" Madison high-fived her cousin.

"Yeah, good work, Olivia," said Zack. "But could you please not do that ever again? You're going to give me a heart attack. . . ."

"Let's get the heck out of here," Ozzie said, then turned to Nadie. "Can you get us back to the coast? That's where we left our plane."

"Yeah," Nadie said. "But it's going to be a little bit of a hike."

CHAPTER

After running through the rain forest and back toward the west coast of Madagascar, all seven of the Zombie Chasers gasped for breath. It wasn't a little hike but a very long and exhausting trek through the deepest part of the jungle. The air was thick and humid, making it hard to breathe. Both of Zack's hamstrings felt like they were about to cramp. He couldn't wait to get back to the plane. The sky had cleared up a bit as the storm clouds headed to the opposite side of the island. Finally, they left the jungle and hurried toward the beach, past a scattering of palm trees. The propeller plane sat about a quarter mile down the coast.

Thankfully, the white sand was free of any undead animals or people. Without any zombies, the beach seemed peaceful, almost like paradise. Zack wished he could lie down and relax. But they didn't have a second to lose. They had to stay on track and get the mayfly sample back to the Caribbean. Nigel Black was waiting for them.

As they approached the aircraft, Zack could hear the plane's communication system blaring from inside the cockpit. It could only be Nigel Black, and Zack hoped that nothing was wrong.

Brrrring! Brrrrring! Brrrring! Ozzie jumped up into the airplane and answered the high-tech face-time walkie-talkie. Zack, then Nadie, then the rest of the kids hopped in after Ozzie and gathered around, listening to the telecom system.

"Hello?" Ozzie said, a little out of breath. "Nigel . . . are you there?"

"Ozzie! Thank goodness." Nigel's voice came through the receiver, and a fuzzy image of him popped onto the screen.

Nigel's face was a bit pixelated, but Zack could still make out his voice. "I've been trying to reach you all day long," Nigel said. "Where were you?"

"We got it! We just got the mayfly sample!" Ozzie said into the speaker. "We're about to head back to you, and soon this will all be over."

"That's great," Nigel said. "Good work, but you can't head back just yet."

"Why not?" Ozzie asked, looking confused.

"While you were gone," Nigel replied, "I ran some tests and made a few calculations with regard to the super zombie virus. . . ." There was something off in his voice, like he didn't want to tell them what he'd discovered.

"Don't even tell me we came all the way to Madagascar for nothing. I was almost eaten by a zombie crocodile!" Zoe said, sticking her face in front of Ozzie and looking directly at Nigel.

"Shush, Zoe." Zack nudged his sister out of the way. "Let the man speak."

"So it turns out that . . . ," Nigel said, clearing his

throat, "we're going to need *one more ingredient* to complete the super zombie antidote."

"What is it?" Madison asked. "What do we need?"

"We're going to need some more ginkgo biloba," Nigel told them. Ginkgo biloba was the extract compound they had been using to knock out zombies. It was kind of like what garlic did to vampires, except one dose of ginkgo and a zombie, or even a super zombie, could be put into a coma for a few hours.

"No problemo," Rice said. "We can just pick some up at the local pharmacy on our way back."

"I'm afraid it's not going to be that easy, Rice," Nigel said. "I'm not talking about just any ginkgo biloba supplement you can buy in the store. We're going to need a portion of the root from an *ancient* ginkgo tree. It's the purest form of the specimen. And that means you're going

to have to travel to China."

"You mean *China*, China?" Olivia asked. "Like, other side of the world China?"

China? Zack's heart plummeted. The only thing Zack knew about China was what he had studied in school. His imagination wandered as Nigel kept talking.

"That's correct," said Nigel. "And you'll have to hurry up. If the mayfly larvae hatch, we won't be able to use it for the antidote. So you'll have to get to China and back in less than a week."

"I once tried to dig to China in the school sandbox," Rice said. "It didn't work out so well."

"We're going to need more fuel," Ozzie said, looking at the gauges on the dashboard.

"I think we can do that," replied Olivia. "Maybe we can find somewhere to fill up?"

"If you don't get slowed down too badly," Nigel said, "you should be able to make it in plenty of time. You have my complete confidence. If anyone can do it, it's you kids."

"I don't understand," Nadie said, butting in. "Why

don't you just bring the mayfly eggs back to him first and then head off for China?"

"There's no time for that!" Nigel replied. "I just ran a brain scan on our super zombie specimen. . . ." He meant Ben, Madison's cousin and Olivia's brother. Ben had been super-zombified when they had mixed the antidote with Spazola Energy Cola at Bunco's Fun World. Nigel continued, "I'm sorry to say, but Ben's symptoms are getting worse."

"But what does that mean, doc?" said Zoe.

"In other words"—Nigel cleared his throat—"it would appear that the super zombies are getting stronger and smarter. They're evolving at an accelerated rate. Have you run into any super zombies abroad?"

"No," said Ozzie. "Why would there be any overseas?"

"How would that even be possible?" said Olivia. "I thought the only super zombies were back in Florida with my parents."

"Those are the only ones we know about," Nigel said. "But you kids proved that to turn a zombie into a super zombie, it only needs to drink that energy cola. And that's a super popular drink all over the world."

"Oh yeah?" Zoe said. "Well, I've got some concerns of my own—"

The connection went fuzzy, and Nigel's voice crackled with static. His image disappeared from the screen.

"Come on!" Rice yelled, smacking the side of their telecom. "What's the matter with this thing?"

The airplane's telecom system blinked again, and Nigel's image came back on the tiny screen.

"Nigel?" Madison said. "Where are we supposed to get this magical ginkgo root?"

"You will be heading to the Zhejiang province

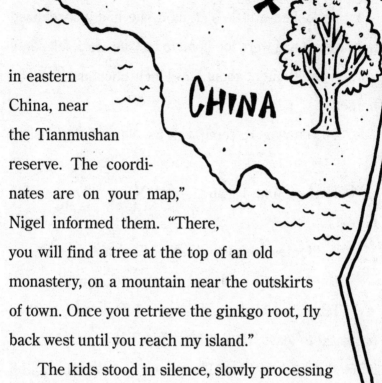

in eastern
China, near
the Tianmushan
reserve. The coordi-
nates are on your map,"
Nigel informed them. "There,
you will find a tree at the top of an old
monastery, on a mountain near the outskirts
of town. Once you retrieve the ginkgo root, fly
back west until you reach my island."

The kids stood in silence, slowly processing
the mission and calculating the dangers that were
now in store for them.

"Well, what are you waiting for?" Nigel shouted
over the line. "Get a move on!" The connection cut
off, and he disappeared from the screen.

Zack and the gang then turned to Nadie.

"So," she said after an awkward silence,

"looks like you guys gotta get going. . . ."

She looked a little sad, as if she had just realized her new friends were too good to be true. Zack felt sorry for her, and thought about how lonely she must be all by herself.

"Do you want to come with us, Nadie?" Zack asked her.

"Thanks, but I can't," said Nadie. "I'm needed here. . . ."

"We'll totes miss you, Nadie!" Zoe said.

"Totes!" Nadie said, and gave everyone a hug.

"Take care of yourself, Nadie," Zack said as they prepared to leave. He felt her whistle in his pocket and handed it back to her. "Thank you for everything," he said, looking her in the eyes. "I promise that after we find the cure for super zombies, we'll come back and unzombify all of Madagascar and the rest of your family."

Nadie held the wooden whistle in her hand. "You should take it," she said. "You have a long journey ahead of you."

"Nah." Zack shook his head. "You need it more than

we do, and besides, I don't think there'll be any lemurs or fossa running around where we're headed."

"Okay," Nadie said, tucking the whistle into her belt. "I guess you're right."

And with that, Zack, Rice, Zoe, Madison, Ozzie, Olivia, and Twinkles waved farewell to Nadie. The propeller plane's engine roared, and soon they took off in search of the ancient ginkgo tree.

A few minutes after takeoff, Zack leaned his head against the back of his seat and drifted to sleep. . . .

He awoke with a jolt and a half-remembered dream. Something about being in a garden filled with exotic flowers. An old man was training him in hand-to-hand combat. A herd of zombies was closing in. He was fighting to the death.

The plane jerked again, and Zack shook back and forth in his seat.

"Everybody buckle up," Ozzie shouted. "Things are about to get a little rough!"

Just then a sound like a buzz saw whizzed through

the cabin and the aircraft bumped from side to side with turbulence.

Glancing out the window, all Zack could see was a dense swirl of sand. His dream forgotten, Zack watched the propellers choke on dust and the back engine pop with an explosion. Black smoke began to rise.

Zack felt his stomach twist as the plane pitched sideways in the wind.

They were going down.

CHAPTER

Ozzie gripped the center stick with both hands, struggling to right the plane, which was out of control, nose-diving toward the ground. For a moment, Zack thought this might be it. He wasn't panicked exactly, as going down in a fiery plane crash might actually be better than getting ripped apart by a bunch of zombies.

Across the cabin, Madison clutched Twinkles to her chest. The scared little pup arfed nonstop. The plane tilted to the side. "Ozzie!" she shrieked. "Please don't let us die, okay?"

"Yeah, seriously!" Zoe shouted. "If I have to die, I'd

rather get zombified and then bite Olivia and become a human again."

"You can't get zombified, Zoe!" Rice said. "You already got unzombified. You're immune!"

"Shoot! I forgot about that," Zoe said, smacking herself on the forehead. "Ozzie, don't you dare crash this plane!"

"Doing my best, guys," Ozzie called back, focused

on bracing the plane through the sandstorm. "Everyone hold on tight!"

Zack felt the plane shift upward and one of the wings dip to the right. He closed his eyes tightly, when suddenly the plane touched down, slightly off-balance. They scraped the ground and fishtailed in the sand before skidding to a bumpy halt somewhere in the middle of the desert.

A sense of calm flowed through the cabin as they all let out a collective phew. Rice was still clinging to Zoe's shoulder with both hands.

Ozzie looked back from the cockpit. "Everyone okay?" he asked.

"I'd be doing way better if this little creepazoid got off me," Zoe said. "Ew, Rice, you're all sweaty. Get away!"

"Rice, are you all right?" Olivia asked.

"I think so," Rice said, testing out all his joints. "Just a little dizzy."

"So we're all good, then?" Ozzie said.

"Think so . . . although, what's the plan now?" Zack asked.

"I'm going to call Nigel and let him know what happened," Ozzie said. He turned to the control panel and tried to use the communication system, but the whole thing was shot. "Uh-oh. Looks like we're on our own . . . and this plane is done for. The engine is out of commission."

Outside, the fierce wind pelted the plane with gusts of sand.

"Great. So, where are we, anyway?" Zack asked.

Ozzie checked the GPS navigation system, which was still working. "We're in Giza," he said. "Near Cairo—it looks like there's an airport there. Maybe we can find another plane."

Zack, Rice, Zoe, and Madison looked at him blankly. Zack was horrible at geography. Whenever it was time to study the world in school, map time turned into nap time.

Olivia stared at the four of them, her eyebrows furrowed incredulously. "Egypt, you guys," Olivia said, "by the Pyramids . . ."

The four kids from Phoenix nodded, their eyes lighting up. "Oh yeah," they all said at once. "I knew that!"

"Sure you did." Olivia rolled her eyes. "Man, you Americans really are bad at geography."

"Well, aren't you just a little miss smarty-pants from Canada," Zoe said.

A few moments later, the sandstorm stopped just as quickly as it had started. Rice stood up and popped open the door. A little bit of sand whisked into the cabin. "I can't believe we landed smack dab in middle of the Pyramids," he said. "How lucky is that?"

"Not that lucky, man," Ozzie said. "The airport's on the other side of the city, and by now Cairo's probably completely zombified."

"Great, then we'll have a chance to check out the Pyramids," Rice said, a hint of wonder in his voice. "One of the seven wonders of the ancient world!"

"Come on, dude," Zack said in the tone he had to

use when Rice was about to make a bad decision. "We have less than a week to get to China and back to the Caribbean—we don't have time for all that!"

"It's all good," Ozzie said, looking at a map in the cockpit. "We have to go past the Pyramids on our way to the airport, anyway."

"Yeah, baby!" Rice jumped for joy and hit his head on the top of the plane. "Ouch!"

"All right then," Zoe said. "Let's get this show on the road." She snatched up the mayfly sample container and led the way into the desert heat.

Everyone followed Zoe. Zack felt his sneakers sink and fill up with sand immediately.

They walked around to the back of the plane and inspected the wreckage. The damage was permanent, the engine still smoking from the midair blowout. It wasn't pretty. As they went around the side, Zack could see that the left propeller was bent and hanging off the wing.

"Soooo, I'm, like, starting to sweat already," Madison said, wiping her brow. "How close are we to the airport?"

"More like how far," Ozzie said. "It's far away, but we should be able to make it. Hopefully we can find some kind of vehicle. Keep your eyes peeled."

"Ugh!" Madison groaned. "If someone finds a car with AC, I'll give them a million dollars."

"You don't even have a million dollars to give," Rice said.

"Yeah, but if I did, I totally would," she said.

Rice pointed up ahead and led the way toward the

Giza Necropolis—a land of the dead pharaohs. The Sphinx and the Pyramids were right in front of them. Despite everything else, Zack had to admit that was pretty cool.

"Arf!" Twinkles chased after Rice.

The hot wind struck them from the northeast and gave them a stinking whiff of rotting flesh. They could hear the undead groans coming from the city of Cairo in the distance. From the sound and smell of it, the capital of Egypt was completely overrun with zombies.

As they passed beneath the giant Sphinx, Zack caught a glimpse of a nearby gift shop for the Pyramid tours. Walking by, he saw something that made his stomach churn and his heart sink with worry. The place was abandoned, but an image in the window showed a large, colorful can of Spazola Energy Cola.

"Guys, check it out," Zack said to the rest of his friends, pointing at the advertisement for the super-zombifying soft drink. "We have to be careful. There could be super zombies around here."

They nodded and proceeded carefully. When they

caught up to Rice and Twinkles, the pair was behind one of the Pyramids, standing over a large rectangular hole in the ground. A staircase led into the desert floor. The area was roped off, with warning signs posted everywhere: DANGER! EXCAVATION IN PROGRESS. DO NOT ENTER.

"Rice," said Zack as he walked up behind his friend. "We have to stick together, okay? We just saw a sign for Spazola. There could be super zombies around here."

"Sorry, man," Rice said. "I just got a little overexcited. . . ."

"I don't understand what you're so excited about," Zoe called to Rice. "It's just a bunch of rocks piled on top of one another . . . whoop-de-do!"

Rice turned and pointed up to the massive structure towering over him. "Pile of rocks? You call that a pile of rocks?" He swept his arm across the view with a grand gesture.

"I mean, I guess it's a pyramid-shaped pile of rocks?" Zoe said, screwing her face up and tilting her head to one side.

"And at least we're in the shade," Ozzie said. The sun was starting to edge toward the west. It'd be dark in a few hours.

"This is where the pharaohs of ancient Egypt were buried," Rice continued. "Well, not really buried, more like mummified. Nobody knows for sure how people built them."

Rice looked down into the blackness of the tomb. "Check out this excavation site. Did you guys know this is near where Nigel was excavating for his TV show? That was over twenty years ago! They must have reopened it recently," he said. "That was where he lost his leg!"

"How do you even know all that?" Olivia asked.

"Because, unlike some of us who shall remain nameless, I didn't just watch every episode of *Unnatural Wonders*, I studied it."

"No wonder that dude's such a weirdo," Zoe said. "Who would want to spend their time in an underground cemetery?"

Rice ignored her. "I read somewhere that the builders were put in secret villages while construction was going on so that no one would know where the pharaoh's treasure was buried. Then the new pharaoh would kill all the builders just to keep the secret safe. . . ."

"That's insane," Ozzie said as they all gathered a little closer.

"Wanna hear something really crazy?" Rice asked. "Some people think that it wasn't even the Egyptian pharaohs and their labor force who built the Pyramids. Some people think that this wasn't done by humans at all but by ancient aliens who came to Earth thousands of years ago and brought super-advanced engineering techniques. How cool would that be?"

"Cooler than standing around while the world gets taken over by super zombies . . . ," Madison said.

"Please tell me you're not one of those people who believes in ancient aliens," Olivia said.

"I would tell you I'm not," Rice said, "but then I'd be a liar."

"Can we leave, please?" Zack tried to interrupt. He was growing more and more anxious to get on with their mission.

"Hold on a second," Madison said. "Who has the mayfly sample?"

Zoe held up the jar. "I got it. We're good to go."

"Wait," Ozzie said. "Put it in Rice's bag. It'll be safer in there."

"Good idea." Rice spun his backpack around on his shoulder. He unzipped the bag and held it open as Zoe stepped forward. "Whoa, Zoe, watch out. There's a scorpion on your foot," said Rice.

"Nice try, skeezball," Zoe sneered. "But I'm not falling for that trick. I invented that trick."

Zack looked down at his sister's shoe and saw a shiny black scorpion perched on the toe of her sneaker, its tail curled over its head like it was about to attack.

"No, seriously," Madison said. "He's not joking around!"

"Huh?" Zoe was about to place the mayfly container in Rice's pack when she looked down and saw the critter on her foot. "EEEEEEEE!" she shrieked and kicked her leg. The scorpion sailed through the air and landed a

safe distance away, but as she freaked out, the larvae jar slipped out of her hand.

Zack's eyes bulged out of their sockets as the container vaulted over their heads and fell into the deep dark pit of the Egyptian catacombs.

Clink-clank-clunk!

Zack listened for the sound of broken glass but heard nothing. He breathed a sigh of relief. Apparently Nigel's fancy jar was made out of expensive plastic.

But even though it was safe, they still had to go get it back.

"I'm so not going down there for that," Zoe said, peering over the scary hole in the ground.

"Cool with me. I'm not afraid of a little adventure,"

Rice said, already making his way down the steps of the excavated tomb. "Check me out. I feel like I'm in my own action movie."

"What would that be?" Zoe asked. *"Idiotic Jones and the Temple of Dumb?"*

"Just make it snappy," Olivia said. "We don't have all day, and this place gives me the creeps."

They all peered over the hole as Rice descended to the bottom of the tomb and disappeared into the shadows.

CHAPTER 7

Zack saw Rice's flashlight click on at the bottom of the black pit. A few seconds later, Rice called up to the rest of them, "I can't find it!"

"What do you mean, you can't find it?" Zack called down. "It couldn't have gone very far. . . ."

"Well, I don't see it, man!" Rice's voice hollered out of the darkness. "Someone come down and help me!"

"Hold on a second, I'll be right down," Zack said to his buddy, then turned to the rest of his friends. "Who's coming with me?"

Zoe and Olivia looked away awkwardly. "Um, we'll keep watch!" Zoe said.

"Now you're going to be a scaredy-cat?" Zack asked his sister.

"Someone has to keep Olivia safe," she replied, and Olivia nodded.

"Yeah, I don't really do the whole haunted-catacombs thing," Olivia said. "Sorry."

"Fine. Me and you, Oz," Zack said. "Let's go."

"Roger that," said Ozzie. "You in?" The two boys looked at Madison.

"Yeah, I guess so." Madison sighed. "I always kind of liked haunted houses anyway. Come on, Twinkles!" She started down the steps, holding Twinkles in her arms. Ozzie followed them down next. Zack turned to Zoe and Olivia.

"Okay, so you guys stay topside and make sure nothing weird happens up here."

"Come on, Zack. Hurry up," said Rice, gazing up from down below.

Olivia made a sour face and pointed down the makeshift staircase at Rice. "Yeah, I'm pretty sure all the weirdness is down there already."

Zack carefully walked down into the catacombs and gulped as he entered the dimly lit tomb.

Rice shone his flashlight in every corner, but there was no sign of the mayfly container. "I don't know what could have happened to it," he said, scratching his head. "We better keep looking. Maybe it rolled down there."

Zack looked "down there" and squinted into the darkness where the light from the flashlight faded away. "Dude, I swear if you're messing with us right now, I'm going to seriously rethink our entire friendship."

"Come on," Rice said. "Why would you think I'd be messing around right now?"

"Because you do it all the time," Madison said, tapping on the flashlight app on her iPhone. "Now let's find this thing and get going. It reeks down here."

The tomb had the musty stink of an attic that hadn't been opened in a decade—and was filled with dead people. The four of them walked slowly, scanning the floor for the mayfly container.

"What's the dealio?" Zoe's voice yelled down from above.

"It's not down here," Ozzie said, looking all around.

"It has to be down there," she said. "I watched myself drop it down there."

Zack called up to his big sis, "Then why don't you come down here and find it yourself?"

"Nah, I'm good," she said. "I trust you guys to find it on your own. Besides, me and Olivia need to keep lookout."

"Whatever," Zack muttered under his breath, as he followed Ozzie, Madison, Rice, and Twinkles farther into the underground tomb.

Zack had never seen anything like this place. It

looked like one of those scary crypt sublevels in a video game. Except this was for real.

The flashlight's beam and the glow of the iPhone illuminated a black spider skittering its way up the wall and vanishing into a jagged crack in the stone ceiling. Zack's heart jumped, and a surge of panic hit his nerves, but he sucked in a deep breath and forced himself to keep walking.

"Hold it," Ozzie said, putting his arm out so that they all stopped in their tracks. Madison and Rice aimed their lights down in front of them, while Zack knelt to examine the dirt-covered floor.

A set of footprints tracked across the ground, one normal shoe print followed by a long streak, as if the second step had an exaggerated limp. *What the . . . ?* Zack thought. *Could there be* zombie mummies *down here? If that was the case, things might be about to get a whole lot worse.* A separate streak squiggled through the dirt, suggesting another object that might have been kicked.

"That could be our mayfly jar," he said. "Looks like it might have gone that way." He pointed in the same direction as the footprints and headed deeper into the catacombs. They followed Ozzie to the end of the hallway, Twinkles trotting behind them. Another corridor connected to their own and they all stood in the center of the intersection. Ozzie glanced down at the ground once more, but the footprints were lost in a jumble of other crisscrossing tracks.

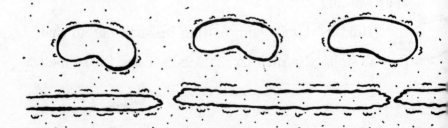

"Which way do we go?" Zack asked.

"Maybe we should split up," said Ozzie.

"No way," Madison said. "Haven't you ever seen a horror movie? Splitting up always ends badly."

A low, gurgling moan came from the shadows, sounding at once far away and right around the corner. Zack could hear the shuffling of feet.

"I want to go whatever way that's not coming from," Rice said.

"This is messed up," Zack said. "The container could be anywhere."

Before they could decide how to proceed, Twinkles took off to the right and made the decision for them.

"Twinkles!" Madison called after her pup, but the little dog wasn't listening. He scampered off, barking into the darkness. Madison darted after him, leaving the boys behind.

"Madison, wait!" Zack shouted.

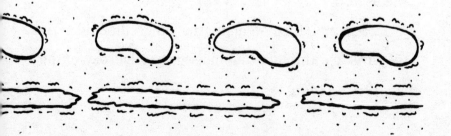

"Shhhh!" Rice said. "There's obviously other people down here, and I'm pretty sure they're not going to be people-people."

"Or mummy-people. Maybe a few archaeologists?" Ozzie said.

"What about zombie mummies?" Rice asked. "What would we even call those? Mummzies?"

"No, zummies!" Ozzie said.

"Good call, man." Rice gave him a high five, although, zummies weren't exactly something to celebrate.

"Will you guys be quiet and help me look for Twinkles?" Madison called back to them. "He went down that way, and I don't see him anymore. . . ."

"Don't worry," Ozzie said, and turned to Zack and Rice. "I'll go help her out. We'll check things out down there. You guys go that way and we'll meet back here in five minutes, okay?"

"Okay," Zack and Rice said, and Ozzie took off after Madison.

Zack and Rice went in the other direction. As they trekked through the underground hallway of the

Egyptian catacomb, Rice began whistling "Whistle While You Work," the tune sung by the seven dwarves in *Snow White*.

"Could you please not whistle right now?" Zack asked, trying to be nice, but it came out harsh.

"Sorry, man. Just trying to lighten the mood," Rice snapped back. They continued in silence when Rice stopped suddenly.

"Did you hear that?"

Zack did. About five feet in front of them came the sound of wheezy, dried-out lungs. The boys froze.

"What the heck was that noise?" Zack asked in the faintest of whispers.

Rice shined the flashlight up and down the catacomb walls. The light waggled down the dark stone tunnel. A blurry figure charged out of the shadows, tottering into the flashlight's beam, and Zack caught a flash of the zombified mummy. Its bandages had started coming off, revealing its decaying flesh. Bones squeaked and muscles crackled at the slightest movement. It was over a thousand years old and it was coming right at them.

"KKRRAWGH!" the mummy zombie rasped, swiping its arms at the boys. Zack ducked just in time before the zummy clawed his face.

Zack came up from a crouch and stared the zummy in the face. The zummy's eyeballs stared at him, googly-eyed in the beam of the flashlight. The decrepit corpse cackled, and Zack swept up his leg with a hard, winding kick, nailing the zummy's shin.

Its shinbone snapped, and it sunk to one leg. Rice hopped forward with a pro-wrestling stomp and shattered the long-dead pharaoh's brittle skull. The skeleton clattered to the floor.

Rice panned the flashlight along the base of the walls, checking every nook and cranny. The light flickered—the battery was low.

"How do you think those mummies are coming back to life?" Zack asked as they walked through an open doorway.

"Maybe the zombies in Cairo got extra hungry?" Rice guessed, stopping on the threshold of an ancient room. The chamber was lined with multicolored, ornate coffins standing erect in neat organized rows, every one of them open.

A few of the Egyptian coffins had been knocked over and damaged. The bodies were gone and trails of slime were dragged all over the place, smearing the floor with undead gunk. This site had obviously been zombified.

But where are all the archaeologists? Zack thought nervously. *Even more important, where are all the mummies? And most important of all: Where the heck is the mayfly larvae container so they could get out of this place?*

Then right on cue, Rice's flashlight browned out and went completely dark.

"Bummer . . . ," Rice said.

Zack lifted his own hand in front of his face. He couldn't see a finger, but he sure could hear the undead groans echoing throughout the pitch-black tomb.

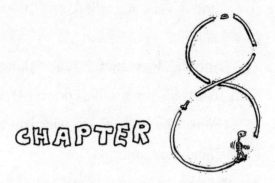

CHAPTER 8

The boys stood totally still, blind in the complete darkness.

"Great," Zack said. "Let's just make our way back and check in with Ozzie and Madison. They should have found Twinkles by now. . . ."

"Yeah," said Rice. "And hopefully the mayfly jar, too."

Reversing through the pitch-dark corridor, the boys retraced their path. Zack led the way with Rice close behind him. The two boys pawed at the walls to guide them through the blackness, taking baby steps. As they neared the intersection of the two corridors Zack and Rice paused.

"Ozzie?" Zack called out into the darkness. "Madison?"

"Shhhh," Rice said. "Quit making noise. We don't want to attract any zombies down here."

"Well, what are we supposed to do?" Zack asked. "Just stand here and wait?"

"Hold it," Rice said. "I just remembered I might have a couple of batteries at the bottom of my backpack."

Zack rolled his eyes. "You just remembered that?"

"Yeah, man, better late than never, right?" Rice said, leaning against the wall while rummaging around in his bag. "And, dude, there's no need to roll your eyes at—"

"How did you know—" Zack started to say when a strange and unexpected noise interrupted him. It sounded like two stone slabs grinding on top of each other. The wall started to move next to him, like a revolving door. And then it stopped as suddenly as it had started.

"Rice, what was that?" Zack asked, but there was no response. "Rice!" he shouted one more time, worried for his best friend. "Can you hear me?"

"Yeah, I can hear you, but you sound like you're really far away!" Rice's voice called through the wall. "These walls must be pretty thick. Can you hear me?"

"Yeah, sort of," Zack said. "What happened?"

"I don't know," said Rice. "I must have hit a trick door or something super cool like that. Not sure, it's

too dark. . . . Hold on. . . . I just found my extra batteries. Phew!"

"You have your flashlight back on?" Zack said. "See if you can activate the door again."

After a moment

Rice called back through the wall. "No go, man. I think it's a one-way door. Feel around on the wall and see if you can flip me back around. Otherwise I'm going to have to find my way back to you from some other route!"

Zack took both hands and groped the wall, feeling for some kind of hidden button or an ancient sconce to pull down like in the movies. But all he felt was the smooth cool surface of stone.

"I can't find it, dude," Zack said, starting to feel panic churn in his belly. "But be careful! I'm going to look for Madison and Ozzie and come get you."

"Watch out for the zummies!" Rice called back, his voice becoming faint in the secret passageway.

All alone now, Zack moved blindly through the corridor, hoping that he was going in the same direction as Ozzie and Madison. He turned a corner, feeling his way with his hands, when a loud growl startled him.

"Twinkles?" Zack said, and tripped backward.

BAM! He landed hard on his butt and hit the back of his head on the floor.

He heard the undead growl again. It definitely wasn't Twinkles.

"ACK!" Zack cried, rubbing the back of his skull. A thin, bony hand reached down, grabbed a fistful of his hair, and lifted him off the ground.

He ripped his head away, losing a tuft of hair in the process. His scalp stung and throbbed, but it was worth it to get free from the zombie. Zack dropped to the ground and crawled through a doorway. He immediately sensed the musty breath of rezombified archaeologists and zumbified mummies. He was surrounded.

Zack couldn't see how many zombies were in the room with him, but he had a feeling it was a whole freakin' lot. A three-fingered claw clamped down on his shoulder and grabbed him from behind. Zack wheeled around and swung blindly at where he thought its head was.

WHAM! His elbow hit its face with a dry crunch. Zack cringed as the crook of his arm got stuck in the zombie's mouth. The corpse's dried-up lip skin crumbled around his elbow joint. He pulled his arm back and his elbow came free from the ancient pharaoh's withered mouth.

Zack felt the bony hand let go of his shoulder and heard the zummy drop to the ground. One down, too many to go.

Zack tried to run but fell to his knees as two hands grabbed his legs. The hands dragged him away from the door and Zack began to panic. How were you supposed to fight a bunch of zombies when you couldn't see where they were coming from?

"Help!" Zack screamed into the black void. "Ozzie! Rice! Madison!" His voice echoed through the tomb. The hands were strong, recently human. He made an educated guess: maybe they belonged to one of the archaeologists.

"Somebody please help me!" Zack cried as the zombie pulled him deeper into the room. Zack reached out, feeling around for something to grab on to. His left hand landed on some kind of stick. Only it wasn't a stick but the shinbone of a zummy. His right hand wrapped around the fleshy ankle of a regular zombie. Zack could feel the clammy skin and the man's coarse leg hair, which was matted with slime.

The zombie kept pulling at his feet, but Zack bent his knees forward and kicked back as hard as he could, bucking off one of the hands. With a little bit of wiggle

room, he kicked even harder a second time. Adrenaline pumped through his veins. The kick landed squarely, and Zack heard an explosion of skin and ancient joints. The sound of bones hitting the floor sent an echo of creepy musical notes throughout the tomb, like the clinking of a wind chime.

His legs were free now, and he tried to stand up, but he felt a dozen arms and hands dangling over him, their slime-slathered fingers tickling his face. Zack flattened himself against the stone floor and ducked under the zombie arms above him. His ears and cheeks were covered in slime. It was like going through a zombie car wash in a convertible. They waved back and forth, slapping him on the sides of his head. Zack crawled forward and jumped to his feet. He tried to remember where the door was and sprinted in that direction.

SMACK! He bashed into something made of solid rock, but it wasn't the wall. It felt like some kind of statue. He reached up and ran his fingers over the sculpture, like a blind person feeling someone's face. It wasn't a statue, he realized. It was one of those standing coffin things that housed mummies. He couldn't think of the word for it. Snuffleupagus? No, a sarcophagus.

The undead mob was closing in. Zack could feel their breath sucking up all his oxygen.

With nowhere else to hide, he pushed over the coffin lid and squeezed in, hoping there wasn't a mummy already inside. Luckily there wasn't. He shut the lid, sealing himself up. He was safe now, but he was also trapped.

Trying to block out the zombie groans right outside, Zack remembered the time when his old nemesis, Greg Bansal-Jones, had shut him in a locker at school. He wished he could go back to that moment. He'd much rather face a couple of school bullies than a

tomb full of zombified mummies.

"HELP!" he yelled, but the snarls of the zummies only grew more intense at the sound of his helpless shout.

Over the subhuman groans, Zack could hear two human voices calling for him. "Zack! Zack! We're coming!" It sounded like Ozzie and Madison! Zack's heart leaped and he yelled back. "Guys, I'm in here. In here, guys! Help, quick!"

CHAPTER

A sliver of light appeared through a crack in Zack's coffin. It was the glow of Madison's smartphone.

"Zack, where are you?" Madison yelled.

"I'm in here," Zack shouted. "Inside the sarcophagus!"

"Inside the wha—" Ozzie cut himself off. "Holy mackerel, there's a lot of zombies in here! Are you really trapped, Zack?"

"No, Ozzie," Zack shouted, his voice thick with sarcasm. "I'm just in the middle of my Houdini routine."

"What happened to Rice?" Ozzie shouted. "Is he with you?"

"I lost him," Zack replied.

"What do you mean, you lost him?" Madison asked.

"What does it matter?" Zack shouted back, frustrated. "Can you just get me out of here?"

"We're on it!" Ozzie yelled.

Zack could hear the clatter of broken jaws, the screech of squeaky joints, the crunch of decayed muscles, and the phlegm-rattling wheeze of the undead mob's rotten breaths.

"It might take a minute," Ozzie said. "There's a freak load of zombies in this place."

"Yeah," Madison said. "Maybe we should lure some of them out. Better than taking them all on at once."

Zack listened as his friends started to distract the zombies away from his sarcophagus.

"Come on, you ugly freakazoids," Madison said in a voice like she was training a new puppy. "This way."

"That's right," Ozzie mimicked. "Be good little brain-munchers."

"Zack, hang in there!" Madison called back. "We'll be back for you in a minute."

Zack could hear the mob leave the room, then

Madison and Ozzie unleash their attack. It was like watching a fight scene with your eyes closed. *Kablam! Pow! BAM!* went the whap of Ozzie's nunchaku. Madison *wah'd* and *hi-ya'd* as she karate chopped. But it sounded like the battle was getting farther away. Zack could barely hear them.

"Hey, guys!" Zack shouted. "Where are you going?" There was still a bunch of zombies outside his sarcophagus, and Zack couldn't escape. Suddenly, his coffin began to rock from side to side. Zack could hear the dry cackle of the zummy trying to push it over.

Wham! The zummy hit the sarcophagus with all its might.

"Whoa!" Zack yelled as the casket crashed to the floor. The lid shifted off the coffin and Zack squirmed out, but then the heavy top moved again and dropped on his ankle. A searing pain shot up his leg and he was stuck.

The zummies were closing in as Zack tried to twist his foot out of his sneaker, but the top of the sarcophagus weighed way too much.

"ACK!" Zack howled.

A flash of light stunned Zack and he glimpsed the most hideously decomposed zummy of all. It towered over him, its face stuck in some kind of permanent yell. It hissed, flashing its brownish-yellow teeth and stretched out its arms, ready to feast on Zack's brain.

WHAP! Another beam of light came from the mummy's head. And just like that, the giant zummy crumpled to the floor.

Zack stared where the mummy zombie had just stood. A shorter, plumper mummy stood over Zack, holding a flashlight. The mummy raised its hand to its face and pulled off its white wrappings.

"'Sup, dude?" Rice said, shining the flashlight up under his chin to make his face look creepy. "Boo!"

"Dude! You scared the crud out of me!" Zack said.

"Sorry, man, but I was just trying to blend in," Rice replied.

"Get me out of here, wouldja?" Zack asked, grimacing.

Rice bent down, lifting the lid of the sarcophagus. Zack freed his ankle and groaned a sigh of relief. He

rolled his ankle around. There'd definitely be a bruise, but at least it wasn't broken. He looked up at Rice. "Where'd you come from?"

"I found my way back. Walked right through the zombies. Had to dodge Ozzie's nunchaku, though. There's a bunch of secret passageways in this joint," Rice told him enthusiastically. "Super cool, right?"

"So you've just been walking around, taking a tour of this place while I've been stuck in this coffin about to get eaten by zombies?"

"Well, first I had to wrap myself in toilet paper

to blend in with the rest of the mummies. I always keep an extra roll in my bag"—Rice winked—"for emergencies."

"Seriously?" Zack shook his head as he rose to his feet.

"I was looking for the larvae jar, too," Rice said defensively. "And I just saved your butt. You owe me."

"Let's go help Madison and Ozzie. They were trying to save me before you showed up—my hero," Zack said sarcastically.

Zack and Rice hurried into the hallway, where half a dozen zombies were still on the attack. Ozzie and Madison were out of breath. It looked like they were having trouble.

"You guys finally decide we deserve a little help?" Madison panted.

Zack spotted a pickax and a shovel leaning against the wall. He ran over and tossed the shovel to Rice, keeping the pickax for himself.

"Hey!" Rice said, making a face. "Why do you get the pickax?"

"Because," Zack said. He swung the pickax at a zummy behind Ozzie.

"Because isn't an answer, Zack," Rice reminded his buddy. He brought the shovel over his head and slammed it down on a zummy's cranium, watching its old brains puff up in a cloud of dust. "I just don't understand why you get the big cool pickax and I have the stupid shovel."

"Fine," Zack said. "You want the pickax? Is that going to make you happy?"

"Nah," Rice said. "I'm good with the shovel."

They finished off the remaining zombies and stood in the silence of the

catacombs, catching their breaths.

"Okay, you guys," Madison said. "We have to find Twinkles. . . ."

"More important," Ozzie said, "we have to find the mayfly jar and get out of here."

"How is that more important than Twinkles?" Madison asked.

"Because the fate of the entire world rests on us finding the mayfly sample and getting it to Nigel Black. . . ."

"Well," she said, "the fate of my world depends on us finding my puppy."

All of a sudden, Zoe's voice rang down, "Hey, bozos! What's taking so long?"

"Oh, I'm sorry," Zack shouted back. "Are we not going fast enough for you? While you sit on your butt and wait for us to defeat an entire underground tomb full of zombies?"

"I'm actually not sitting on my butt, I'm standing on my feet," Zoe said. "But seriously . . . we gotta jet."

"Awesome!" Ozzie called up to them. "You guys found another jet?"

"No, dummy, you think we just randomly found another plane?" she said.

"I don't know," Ozzie said. "You just said you got a jet."

"I said we have got to jet," Zoe said, speaking slowly, as if to an infant. "As in, we have to go. Like now."

"Seriously, guys," Olivia said. "There's a whole freakin' army of zombies heading our way!"

"Yeah, and it's super hot up here," Zoe added.

"We can't go anywhere yet!" Zack shouted back. "We don't have the mayfly jar."

"Okay, now you're all just getting on my nerves," Zoe bellowed. "Get out of that tomb this instant!"

"Not without the mayfly jar!" Zack shouted.

"And not without Twinkles, either!" Madison yelled.

"You mean you lost Twinkles, too?" Zoe asked in disbelief. "What kind of operation are you guys running down there?"

"We didn't lose Twinkles," Ozzie said. "We just haven't seen him in a while."

"Well, you're not going to be seeing anything if we don't get out of here," Zoe said. "Because these zombies are going to eat your eyeballs out of your heads."

"She's right—we have maybe, like, two minutes to find Twinkles and those mayfly larvae," Olivia said, "or else we're going to be mincemeat for these zombie freaks!"

"Come on, you guys," Zack said, trying to rally the troops. "Let's do this. . . ."

The four of them walked up and down the dark hallway, scanning the floor for the mayfly container.

"Twinkles!" they called. "Twinkles!"

Just then Twinkles appeared out of the shadows and sprinted to Madison.

"Oh, Twinkles." Madison bent down to scoop up her pup. "Thank goodness you're all right!"

"That's great, Madison," Rice said. "But we still don't have the mayfly jar."

"Umm, yeah, we do," Madison said. "Twinkles has it in his mouth!"

Zack, Rice, and Ozzie all cheered. "Woo-hoo!"

"Jinx!" Rice shouted, and gave them each a slap on the shoulder.

"Come on, losers!" Zoe shouted. "I don't plan on getting torn to pieces on account of your super slowness!"

Zack took the special mayfly container from Madison and put it in Rice's backpack. He was ready to leave these zumbified catacombs behind for good.

CHAPTER

ack above ground, things went from bad to worse. Immediately, Zack could see what Zoe and Olivia were worried about—an endless mass of zombies headed straight toward them. There were thousands upon thousands of them. The late afternoon sky was filled with kicked-up dust from the foot-dragging lunatics.

"Where did they all come from?" Zack asked.

"Cairo's a big city," Ozzie said. "The whole place must be zombified by now."

"Which means we're probably the only human brains in the vicinity," Rice pointed out.

"So, which way is the airport?" Olivia asked. "We have to get a new plane."

Ozzie pointed directly at the zombies. "Across the Nile, and all the way on the other side of the city."

"We need some kind of transportation," Madison said. "We're never going to make it on foot."

Zack glanced around, but knew they'd never find a car in the middle of the desert.

"What are we going to do?" Zoe said.

"Listen up, you guys," Zack said, cupping his hand around his ear.

Over the groans of the undead, Zack heard an animal—it sounded like something between a cow's moo and a horse's whinny, and it was coming from near one of the smaller pyramids.

"Did you guys hear that?" Zack asked, walking toward the sound. "Over here."

The kids raced to the side of the pyramid, where they saw three healthy-looking camels. They were tied to a wooden post, their owners nowhere in sight.

"Wow, I can't believe they're not zombies!" Rice said. "I guess we found our ride."

"Anyone ever ridden a camel?" Ozzie asked.

"I've ridden horses before," Madison said.

"Me, too," said Olivia.

"Good, it's basically the same thing," Ozzie told them. "Except camels are a little lazier. And like to bite and spit."

"It's better than walking," Zoe said. "Let's roll. . . ."

Olivia and Madison mounted one of the camels, siting on either side of its hump. Madison took the reins, holding Twinkles in her other hand. Ozzie and Rice hopped up on the second camel, with Ozzie in front. Zack and Zoe took the last one. Zack had to lift his foot up to chest level just to get it in the stirrup. He had no idea camels were so tall. The camel snorted, obviously grumpy.

"Come on, little bro," Zoe said. "You can do it!"

"Could you gimme a hand at least?" Zack asked.

"What do you say?"

"Please?" Zack grunted.

"Please what?"

"Pretty please with sugar on top?" Zack was about to fall.

"And what else?"

"Pretty please with sugar on top and sprinkles and chocolate sauce and gummy bears . . ."

Zoe considered this for a moment. "Yeah, I guess that sounds pretty good." She reached down and helped her brother onto the camel's back.

"Giddyup, camel!" Madison ordered, and slapped the reins. Ozzie and Zoe copied her, and all three camels started to trot.

Zack and the gang rode straight into the crowd of mutants. The camels began to pick up speed as they moved through the zombie mob. Zack raised his leg to kick one of the zombies. "I don't think these camels know what *giddyup* means!" Zoe jabbed the camel with her heel. "Come on, slowpoke, run!"

The camels sped up, and they were halfway through the swarm.

Ozzie swung his nunchaku like a knight crusading into battle, knocking out anything in their path. Zoe blasted a zombie in the face with the sole of her sneaker and popped a swollen blister on its face with a splat. Madison and Olivia's camel was keeping up,

but Ozzie and Rice were trapped by a horde of zombies. Sand whipped into Zack's face as he squinted at something behind them. A dark brown camel raced at their rear.

Someone else was riding a camel.

A zombie can ride a camel? Zack thought.

The rider had on a dark gray robe.

It looked pale.

Wrinkly.

That ain't no zombie, Zack thought, *that's a super zombie!*

He called out to his friends. "Guys! Super zombie! Five o'clock!"

Rice couldn't hear Zack over the crowd. "What?" he asked.

"Super zombie!"

Zoe nudged Zack with her elbow. "Quit yelling in my ear, I'm trying to concentrate."

Zack growled in frustration. The super zombie was gaining on them. "Super zombie!" Zack yelled at the top of his lungs.

But it was too late.

"Olivia!" Zoe yelled. "Look out!"

"Growlghk!" The super zombie lunged for Olivia.

It grabbed her by the arms and dragged her backward onto his camel.

"Ahhhhh!" Olivia shrieked, surprised by the sneak attack.

Zoe, Rice, and Madison all sprang into action and raced their camels toward Olivia.

"It must know she's the cure!" Zack yelled. "These super zombies just don't give up, do they?"

"Help me!" Olivia cried.

"We're coming for you, Olivia. Don't let go!" Madison called, and Twinkles barked.

But the super zombie was already getting away, heading into the city. The Zombie Chasers tried to make their camels go faster, but soon their friend had disappeared from sight on the back of the camel.

"If we lose her, this is all over," said Zack. "Let's go, team!"

The zombie swarm thinned out as they neared Cairo. But their camels slowed down to a walk and then stopped completely. One of the camels sat down and slumped over.

"Ummm . . . ," Zoe said. "Our camel just, like, quit on us."

"Uh-oh." Rice pointed to the camel's leg. "That's no good."

Zack saw that the camel's foot was bleeding.

"Your camel's hurt, too!" Zoe said, pointing to Rice and Ozzie's.

The camel had a deep gash in its flank and a moment later dropped to a heap in the sand. Madison's camel fell over, too, suffering from a bite wound in the right shoulder.

All the camels had been bitten by zombies.

The kids jumped off and ditched the zombifying camels.

"Come on! If we don't hurry, we're never going to find Olivia." Madison took off, sprinting down the street where the super zombie disappeared.

They ran through the marketplace, which was teeming with zombies, bowls of rotting fruit, and colorful dresses stained with zombie slime. Buckets of spices were dumped on the ground, and carpets and tapestries had been knocked all over the place.

At the center of the bazaar a white van with tinted

windows was parked with its door wide open and its key in the ignition.

"Looks like we've got a getaway car," Rice said.

"There's not going to be any getaway," Madison said. "Not until we find Olivia."

"Hey, check it out," Zoe said. "Those look like camel tracks. We should probably follow those, right?"

As they all followed the super zombie's camel tracks, Zack noticed the white van starting to jostle and shake. "Hey, guys, that's not our getaway van. That's the super zombie's escape plan! Get it!"

As Zack sprang into action, the white van reversed toward them, and the super zombie driver looked at them and cracked a smile.

The van vroomed, kicking up a cloud of sand in Zack's face, but he was running full speed. He caught up to the van as it skidded in the dirt and he leaped onto the back bumper, grabbing hold of the rack on top. He caught his balance as the super zombie getaway van swerved left and right and left again. Holding on tight with his right hand, Zack reached down with his left and tested the door handle. It clicked and popped open, and he ducked inside.

Olivia was tied up in the backseat with a dirty sock stuffed in her mouth. The super zombie kidnapper was up front, both hands clutched on the steering wheel, driving like an absolute psycho.

Zack pulled the sock out of Olivia's mouth and started to untie her.

Olivia spat. "*Putoohey!* Thanks, Zack! This dude's a total sicko. . . ."

Zack was pulling at the knots around Olivia's wrists when a huge hand snagged him by the shirt collar and pulled him up toward the front of the van.

Zack nailed his funny bone on the radio dials and static blared through the speakers. The super zombie sneered at Zack, who managed to squirm away. Zack brought his elbow back and swung it, nailing the super zombie's head. But its skull was too hard and the undead freak only grunted louder, angrier. Its arm shot out and it clasped its pale white hand around Zack's throat.

"I can't breathe, you freakin' psychopath," Zack

wheezed. "Let me go!" But the super zombie wasn't letting go. Its grip was getting tighter.

Zack tried to suck in air but got nothing. He kicked with his feet, and almost drilled the super zombie in the face but missed. The sole of his sneaker caught some traction on the steering wheel and the van jerked wildly to the right.

"Ahhhhhh!" Zack hollered as they went careening off the side of the road and crashed into a wooden telephone pole.

WHAM-CRACK!

Zack went flying into the dashboard and the super zombie smashed headfirst through the windshield. Zack lifted his head up, gasping for air. Olivia crawled up from the backseat, her hands still tied together as the rest of the gang ran over to the car wreck.

"Whoa! That was crazy," Ozzie said. "Are you both okay?"

"I will be as soon as someone unties me," Olivia said.

"I'm good," Zack said, cracking his neck as he sat in the passenger seat. "Sort of."

"You guys, we gotta get out of here," Madison said. "There's a buttload of regular zombies closing in on us."

"We have to get rid of that first." Zack pointed to the super zombie with its head through the windshield.

Ozzie, Zoe, Madison, and Rice all grabbed part of the passed-out super zombie and wriggled its head out of the busted glass, then tossed it out of the van.

They all hopped in and slammed the doors shut. Zoe turned the key in the ignition and the engine sputtered and died. "Come on, don't do this."

Zack looked out the windows as a gigantic herd of brain-cravers tottered around the van.

"Let's go, Zo," Zack shouted to his sister. "Get us out of here!"

Zoe turned the key again, and the engine sputtered, then rumbled to life. She shifted into reverse and backed up into a dense mob of undead ghouls, who pawed at the back windows, trying to scrape their way inside.

The zombie moans were deafening, coming from every direction.

"Whoa! Watch out!" Rice yelled from the back as

a wooden telephone pole toppled and the power lines snapped. The post landed on a pile of undead mutants and the thick black wires danced through the crowd, zapping them all with a huge electric shock.

"Go, go, go!" Ozzie yelled at Zoe and she floored the gas, zooming away from the electroshocked zombie swarm.

Zoe swerved through the undead and then slammed the accelerator again as they shot out of Cairo and sped for the airport.

The sun was setting as they passed abandoned buildings and wove through stray zombies. The twilight cast a weird light on the city and made everything feel like a waking nightmare. Zack was grateful when they finally arrived at the runway and found a working plane. It even had enough gas to get them to China.

"Okay, we're taking off in T minus ten minutes," Ozzie said as he warmed up the engine.

Zack let out a sigh of relief.

They were on their way again.

CHAPTER  11

Flying over China, Zack gazed out the window of the airplane. The sky was a crisp blue and the morning sun beat down.

After leaving Egypt, they'd jetted forward for twelve hours, following the coordinates Nigel had given them. They were heading for Hangzhou, where they would find the ancient ginkgo tree at the kung fu temple.

Zack could make out the Great Wall snaking through the mountains. He squinted, and thought that he could make out a mass of zombies crawling all over the gigantic fortress. But the plane was too high up for him to tell for sure, and it was possible that his mind was playing tricks on him. He hadn't been able to sleep the entire flight, sitting up in the copilot's seat next to Ozzie. Zack wished he had gotten a little shut-eye.

The rest of his friends reclined in the passengers' seats, snoring away. Even Ozzie was out like a light. He had put the plane on autopilot and given Zack strict instructions to wake him up in case of any emergency or when they were close to their destination.

So Zack couldn't fall asleep even if he wanted to. Plus, the last time he dozed off on the way to Egypt, he'd dreamed about super zombies attacking him. If he couldn't even get away from zombies by falling asleep, then he preferred to stay awake.

But Zack let his friends sleep. Only an hour and a half remained on their flight time, and if they were going to survive in the most zombified country in the world, they were going to need everyone as well rested as possible. And if the super zombie virus had spread to China as well, then getting to the ginkgo root was going to be extra dangerous.

* * *

Zack and the gang touched down at the airport in Hangzhou, which was pretty close to the ancient ginkgo tree—the final ingredient they needed for the super zombie antidote.

Ozzie parked the plane on the runway and opened the door. They hurried out of the airport and followed the directions Nigel had given them. Zombies were everywhere.

"Over there!" Olivia shouted, pointing at a couple of golf carts at the outskirts of a massive traffic jam.

They sprinted through the abandoned cars and hopped in the carts. Zack got behind the wheel. He had driven one of these things before when his dad had taken him golfing, plus he was pretty good at the go-kart track.

He shifted the golf cart into gear and hit the gas. Rice and Madison hung on tight as they zipped off toward the city of Hangzhou. Zoe, Ozzie, and Olivia rode in the cart next to them.

As they zoomed through the city streets, Zack looked up and saw a humongous billboard flashing over their heads: Spazola Energy Cola!

"Guys," Zack said, "be on the lookout for super zombies. They could be anywhere."

"And they're probably going to try to kidnap Olivia again," Rice said.

The city of Hangzhou was long and narrow, running

alongside a peaceful river. The two golf carts whizzed down the highway and into the city proper.

The undead masses shuffled across the pavement, dripping slime from every wound and orifice. The entire city was completely zombified. Undead men, women, and children filled every corner.

"We have to get out of here, you guys!" Ozzie called over the zombie grunts.

"Let's go!" Rice shouted. "The temple should be that way!" He pointed toward a bridge by the river, which led away from the zombie-infested city.

They traveled down a maze of narrow roads, till they reached the temple, where the ancient ginkgo tree was said to grow.

The temple was at the top of a steep cliff, surrounded by a bright-green bamboo forest that swayed slightly in the wind.

Up a very long stone staircase, Zack could see the pagoda, made up of three ornamental towers. In front of the temple was a courtyard planted with smaller trees and bushes.

"That's gotta be it, guys," Zack said with a smile. "We made it!"

They approached the step and noticed a man sitting with his legs crossed. Zack did a double take—that dude definitely hadn't been there a minute ago.

"You must be the Zombie Chasers," the man said in slightly accented English. "My name is Zhang Wu. I knew you would come."

"Did Nigel call you or something?" Rice asked.

"I do not know this Nigel you speak of," Zhang said. "But I knew you would be here. In this moment."

Zack's eyes widened as he stared at the man's face, his long beard and bushy eyebrows. The man wore a long, dark robe that tied at the waist. Zack had seen his face before somewhere, but couldn't quite place it. And then it dawned on him. He had never met the man in person, but he had seen him in his dream. *The kung fu master*, Zack thought. He couldn't believe it, and yet there he was.

CHAPTER 12

"How did you know we would come?" Rice asked.

"I dreamed it," the man said, and then looked at Zack. "You remember, don't you, Zachary?"

"What's he talking about, Zack?" Zoe asked her brother.

"I had a dream on the plane when we were flying into Cairo," Zack explained. "I was training to fight off a bunch of super zombies and I had a kung fu master teaching me. My master was . . . it was . . . him." Zack nodded to the old Chinese man.

"But how is that possible?" Madison asked. "How

can you have a dream about someone you've never met before?"

Zack was stumped. He had no idea, but before he even tried to answer the question, the old man spoke.

"There are untold mysteries in this world," Zhang Wu said. "And some of them have no logical answer. The important thing is that you made it here, and now you must fulfill your destiny." The old man pointed up the steps to the temple. "In the garden of the temple is the ancient ginkgo tree you seek."

"Awesome, mister, thanks for the help," Ozzie said. He then brushed past the kung fu master and headed for the steps leading up to the temple.

"Not so fast, my young pupil," the kung fu master said. "You are not ready to ascend those steps."

"But you just said the ginkgo tree is up there, right?" Ozzie asked.

"I did," said Zhang Wu. "But I did not say you were ready to receive its magic."

"Whatever, man." Ozzie brushed off the kung fu master. "Come on, you guys! Let's go get this ginkgo root and then head back to Nigel."

In a flash Zhang Wu bent his knees and jumped into the air, executing a perfect backflip. He landed between Ozzie and the first stair. "I don't think you understand my meaning, young one."

"Well, then why don't you stop talking in these backward riddles?" Ozzie said to the master.

"Hey, Ozzie," said Zack. "Maybe not such a good idea to talk back to this guy, huh? I mean, after all, he was kind of in my dream and stuff."

"Let me handle this, Zack," Ozzie said without taking his eyes off Zhang. "This is between me and him."

"I think you should listen to your friend's advice," said Zhang. "It is not wise to defy your master."

"Please, you're not my master," Ozzie

said. "I studied with Wong Fei Li when my dad was stationed in Japan. And there's nothing you can do that's going to stop us from going up those steps and getting that ginkgo root."

"And I say there is," said Zhang very calmly.

"Then you're about to get a rude awakening, pops." Ozzie struck a martial arts stance and pulled out his nunchaku, ready to do battle.

"Come on, you guys," Madison said. "This is silly. You don't have to do this."

"With all due respect, young lady," said Zhang, "I think your friend here needs to learn a lesson."

"I don't learn lessons, old man," Ozzie said with fire in his eyes. "I teach them."

"Come on, you two. Enough of all this macho stuff," Olivia said. "There's got to be a way we can work this out."

"I am working it out, Olivia," said Ozzie.

"It's okay," Zoe said, placing

her hand on Olivia's shoulder. "Let's just let the boys do their stupid little boy thing."

Standing next to Rice, Zack felt his buddy nudge him in the rib cage. "This is going to be awesome," he whispered to Zack. Then he shouted, "Go get 'im, Oz!"

"Don't worry, fellas," Ozzie said with confidence. "This'll all be over soon enough."

And he was right.

Ozzie sprang forward, his nunchaku a dizzy blur. Zack watched his friend as he charged at the kung fu master. In a split second, Zhang Wu shot his left arm out toward Ozzie. Then, with a dainty little flick of his wrist, he sent Ozzie flying into a tree trunk.

"Ozzie!" the whole group shouted as they ran over to their fallen friend.

"Are you okay, man?" Rice asked, kneeling.

Ozzie nodded his head weakly. He pushed himself off the ground and rubbed his back.

Rice turned and glared angrily at Zhang Wu. "What'd you do to our Ozzie?"

"I taught him a lesson," said Zhang. "And I would

like to teach you all a lesson. I do not wish to fight you. I
wish to train you."

"Dude, we don't have time for all that," Zoe said.
"We've got to get that ginkgo tree root back to the
Caribbean before our mayflies go bad!"

"And in order to do that," said Zhang, and then he
paused.

"In order to do that what?" Zoe asked.

"In order to do that . . . ," Zhang repeated with a
blank stare.

"Is this guy having a stroke or something?" Olivia asked. "Sir, are you feeling all right?"

"In order to obtain the root of the ginkgo and save the human race . . ." Zhang paused one more time before finishing his sentence. "You must be strong, you must be brave, but above all else, you must BE the zombie. . . ."

"Is this guy for real?" Madison asked. "Zack, are you sure you're not dreaming?" She reached out and pinched the back of his arm.

"Ow!" Zack shouted. "Too hard!"

"What?" Madison said. "I just wanted to be sure."

"Are you ready to listen to me now?" Zhang said to them.

They stared at him.

"Yes or no?" Zhang changed his tone from calm to not so calm.

Zack looked at his friends and shrugged. "I think we ought to hear him out."

"I don't think we have another choice," Rice said. "Besides, it might be kind of awesome to get coached by this dude. Did you see what he just did to Ozzie? Sorry, man, but he totally kicked your butt."

Ozzie slanted his eyebrows, glaring at Rice as he brushed the dirt off his shoulders.

"And if you don't want to get your own butts kicked, as you put it, then you will come with me where it is safe," Zhang told them. "As we speak, there are thirty of your so-called super zombies guarding the ginkgo tree. Like me, the super zombies knew you would be coming."

"How did they know that?" Zack asked.

"I'm not sure," Zhang said. "But they grow smarter by the day."

Ozzie straightened up and gave his neck a good crack. He looked at Zhang and said, "If you think we're scared of a few super zombies, then you don't know us very well."

"These are no ordinary super zombies," Zhang said. "They were my disciples, all thirty of them, and they became infected with the zombie virus. I kept them locked in the temple, but they were accidentally exposed to that awful beverage Spazola Energy Cola. Now they are all super zombies. Super zombies trained in the art of kung fu. If we are going to have any chance of defeating them, and getting your ginkgo root, then we must begin your training immediately."

"Well, why didn't you just tell us that in the first place?" Olivia asked, frustrated.

"The past is behind us now, and we mustn't dwell in it," Zhang Wu said with a flip of his long white beard. "Come with me. . . . It isn't safe for us to be here any longer."

CHAPTER 13

ack, Rice, Madison, Zoe, Olivia, and Twinkles followed Zhang Wu away from the temple and down a narrow dirt track. He led them through a lush garden filled with exotic plants and flowers—that Zack recognized from his dream—until they reached a small hut. It was hidden from view by the thick greenery.

Behind the shack was a training center set up in the dirt yard. There were wooden posts stuck in the ground and racks full of martial arts weaponry.

Zhang Wu walked them out to the training yard and ordered them to line up single file. The six of them obeyed and watched their new kung fu teacher pace back and forth.

Since finding out about the super zombies that guarded the ginkgo tree, Zack had a sick, panicked feeling in his gut. He didn't want to interrupt, but he needed answers. He couldn't help raising his hand, like he was in class.

"I see you have a question," Zhang said. "Questions are for later. Let us begin."

Zack hated when adults cut him off when he had something important to say. His teachers did it all the time. "It's just . . . ," he began anyway, "how did the super zombies know we were going after this particular ginkgo tree?"

"I've told you already I do not have the answer," Zhang said with growing impatience.

Rice turned and looked at Zack. "Why? Do you think maybe they got to Nigel? Maybe that's why we couldn't get through to him in Egypt?"

"I don't see how else they could have known," said Zack. "Do you?"

Rice racked his brain for another possibility. "If they have Nigel, what are we going to do?"

"It's not the end of the world," Ozzie said. "We still have a sample of the giant frilled tiger shark digestive enzyme, the mayfly larvae, and Olivia. We could create the antidote ourselves as a last resort."

"Yeah but maybe not enough of it," Zack said.

"Okay, so maybe it is the end of the world," said Ozzie.

"Guys, don't go jumping to conclusions," Zoe said. "Maybe they sent a spy or something and were eavesdropping on our plan."

"It doesn't matter why they know about the ginkgo tree," Olivia added, a little annoyed. "The point is they're here, and we have to get past them. So let's just listen up to Zhang. After all, it's my family who got super-zombified. Got it?" She turned to the kung fu master, who was meditating on the floor with his eyes closed. He'd ignored the entire argument. "Take it from here, Zhang."

Zhang Wu's eyes flicked open and he went from sitting to standing in the blink of an eye. His expression changed to a scowl as he gave them a good once-over, looking them up and down.

Zack, Rice, Ozzie, Madison, and Zoe all straightened up and went quiet. Even Twinkles snapped to attention and faced the kung fu teacher. Zhang nodded at Olivia and then continued.

"Now, where was I?" Zhang tried to get his train of thought back.

"You were going to teach us how to BE the zombie," Rice said.

"Right, but, like, here's the thing, Zhang," Zoe said. "We've all *been* zombies before. Except for Olivia."

"Yeah," Madison said. "She's a vegan and the regular zombie antidote. She's also my cousin."

Zack looked at Ozzie. Ozzie knew better than to test Zhang's patience. *Guess he learned his lesson*, Zack thought, following Ozzie's lead and staying quiet, too.

"So, what she's saying is—and correct me if I'm wrong, Zoe," Rice said, "we're just not sure we don't already know what you have to teach us."

Zhang Wu's mouth curled into a frown and his eyes

narrowed at Rice. "You!" he snapped. "You like to exercise your mouth but not the rest of your body, eh? . . . Down on the ground! Fifty push-ups! Now!"

"Hah!" Zoe let out a loud chuckle.

Zhang shot Zoe a sharp, cutting glance. "What is so funny?"

"There's no way he can do fifty push-ups," she said. "Look at him!"

Rice looked at Zhang sheepishly. "She's right. I can't. I could maybe do, like, five or six, tops. . . ."

"Very well," said Zhang. "You do your five, and she can do the other forty-five."

"Hey!" Zoe cried. "That's not fair!"

"And since when have you ever known the world to be fair?" Zhang said. "Push-ups now!"

Zoe rolled her eyes as she got down in push-up position next to Rice. "This guy's a real stickler, huh?"

About a minute later Zoe had knocked out her set of push-ups. Rice was still on his third.

"Pathetic . . . ," Zhang muttered to himself, shaking his head while Rice finished up. "I see we have a lot of

work to do. . . . Ozzie, please step forward and face the group. Am I to believe that I can trust you to lead your friends through a warm-up routine?"

"Sir, yes, sir!" Ozzie barked.

"Very good," Zhang said. "Show them the basics. Work them out for half an hour and then come inside for supper. You all look like you could use a decent meal."

Zhang then left them to their exercises.

"Okay, guys, you heard the man," Ozzie said, striking a wide stance. "Follow me. Like this."

Zack mimicked Ozzie's pose and Ozzie began the kung fu warm-up.

"Ho!" he grunted and punched with his right hand. "Again!" Ozzie commanded.

"Arf!" Twinkles echoed, wagging his tail by Ozzie's feet.

Zack and his friends punched with their lefts. "Ho!"

"Again!"

After they finished their exercises, the kids all gathered inside. Zhang had bowls of white rice waiting for them, along with fresh fruit from the garden. Zack and the group sat down at the round table and began to eat. It had been a long day, and they were all famished.

"Hey, check it out." Madison giggled, watching Rice gobble up his bowl of steaming hot rice. "Rice is eating himself."

"Mmmm," Rice said. "I taste delicious. . . ."

They all laughed and then scarfed down the rest of the meal. When they were done, Zhang pointed to the doorway off the main room. "Bunk beds are in there. Rest up. Training continues tomorrow."

Tomorrow came and went and turned into the next day and then the next. In the span of seventy-two hours,

Zhang had given them a crash course in kung fu, teaching them the fundamentals of all five animal fighting styles: crane, dragon, monkey, snake, and tiger.

He showed them how to handle the four major martial arts weapons: the nunchaku (which Ozzie had demonstrated), the mace (which was basically a big metal club), the bo staff (a long stick, which they were all pretty good at), and rattan sticks (two shorter rods, which everyone was pretty bad at). Edged weapons were not allowed, which meant no samurai swords. They could not fatally wound the super zombies. After all, they were Zhang's

disciples and to Zhang they were family. He wanted to save them, too.

At the end of the third day,

Zhang lined them up and looked them over. Zack even thought he saw the old master crack a smile.

"I believe we are making some progress," Zhang said. "But you're forgetting our core principle. You must BE the zombie."

Zack kicked the dirt in frustration. "You keep saying that," he said, "but you never tell us what it means."

"You will know when you are ready to know," Zhang said. He then walked away and headed into the hut to prepare their meal.

When he was gone, the group huddled up and Zack looked in the eyes of each and every one of them. "I'm getting a little worried," he said. "We don't have many more days to waste training with this guy."

"I don't think it's been a waste," Madison said. "I feel much more toned than I have in a while, and he's got fresh fruit from the garden. So yummy!"

"Okay, but if we don't get that ginkgo root back to Nigel in the next forty-eight hours, the mayfly larvae will be useless."

"Plus, he keeps talking about 'being the zombie,'" said Rice. "We've been at this for three days now, and I don't feel any wiser or more zombielike. I mean if he really wants us to be like a zombie, we might as well go eat someone's brains."

"That's totes McGross, Rice," Madison said. "Yuck!"

"I think he's talking about getting into the mindset of the super zombies, not actually being one," Olivia said.

"Who knows what this guy's talking about," said Zoe. "I'm sure he's a great kung fu master and all, but I'm starting to think he's a little bit cuckoo."

"I'm with Zoe on this one," Ozzie said. "I think we're ready to go fight these guys. If he wants to come, great! But if he says we're not ready, I say we go get the ginkgo root tonight, with or without him."

"All in favor say aye," Zack said.

Everyone put their hands in the middle of the huddle. "Aye!"

The kids gathered around the table for dinner. Zack sat in his seat, trying to think of a way to bring up that they were done training with Zhang. He wasn't sure how to broach the subject, but it had to be done. They were running out of time.

"Excuse me, Zhang?" Zack called to their kung fu trainer in the kitchen. "We really appreciate all this training and food you've been giving us, but we all feel like we're ready to take on the super zombies. . . ."

"That would not be wise at this juncture," said Zhang. "Your training is not complete."

"Be that as it may," Zack said, "we don't have a lot of time. You see, it's a long way back to the Caribbean and we've got that mayfly sample and well . . . we kinda gotta get going."

Without responding, Zhang set down a platter of some new kind of food that none of them had ever seen before—thick slices of meat slathered in a brown sauce.

Zack scrunched his face at the meal, looking confused.

"What is it?"

"Monkey brains," said Zhang. "A delicacy. Go on, eat up!"

"There's no way I'm eating that," Zoe said.

"I can't eat that," Olivia said. "I'm the antidote." It was the first time Zack had ever seen her happy about that fact. Both girls stood up from the table and walked to the bunk room.

"I think I'm going to be sick," Madison said, pushing her seat away from the table and leaving the room.

"I don't need to eat brains to fight zombies," Ozzie said. "Do you think the zombies are up there eating rice and fruit so they can BE like us? Excuse me. . . ." Ozzie rose and left the table.

Zack and Rice were the only ones left. They looked up at Zhang, who was waiting patiently for them to start eating.

"This is going to make us ready to take on the super zombies?" Rice asked.

Zhang gave them a nod, gesturing toward the meal.

Rice shrugged and served up two helpings of the monkey brains, one for Zack and one for himself. Zack looked down at his plate. It didn't smell so bad, but knowing what it was made his stomach turn.

The boys dug in for their final round of zombie training. Rice wolfed his down, and Zack took a nibble, too.

"Hmm, that's not so bad," Zack said. "Tastes kind of like chicken. . . ."

Rice chewed and chewed, talking with his mouth full. "I mean, it's a little tough, but I think I kind of get the whole wanting-to-eat-brains thing. It's got a pretty nice flavor."

Once they had finished cleaning their plates, Zack looked up at Zhang again. "So, now you'll take us to go fight the super zombies?"

"Yes," said Zhang. "When you have finished your training."

"But you just said eating this would make us ready," Zack said, his patience wearing thin.

"I believe I said you will be ready when you are ready," Zhang told him and walked off.

Zack and Rice both stormed into the bedroom, and Zack slammed the door behind them. The other four— Ozzie, Olivia, Zoe, and Madison—were sulking on their bunk beds.

Twinkles was in the kitchen, eating the rest of the monkey brains.

Zack stared at his friends. "That dude just made me eat monkey brains for no reason," he said. "Tonight, after he's asleep, we're taking our weapons and storming that temple."

Zoe looked at Zack with what almost could have been considered pride. "Right on, little bro. Let's do this thing."

CHAPTER 14

And so it was decided.

The six of them lay in their bunks, fake sleeping, until they could hear the high-pitched snoring of Zhang Wu. That was the signal for them to quietly slip out from under the covers and creep to the window of their room.

They dropped off the windowsill and then darted across the training yard.

Adrenaline coursed through their veins as they climbed up the temple steps. They were all a little anxious, but their nerves were steady. Leading the way, Zack looked up at the top of the mountain. A figure flashed in the moonlight. It had a shiny bald head and wore an orange kung fu uniform. Its skin looked crinkled and pale, and its eyes were bloodshot. As the figure patrolled the temple, Zack also noticed its arms hanging low out of their sockets, down to the knees, and it seemed to be breathing heavily out of its mouth. Definitely a super zombie.

"Shhhh . . . ," Zack said, and motioned for them to hop off the stairs. They ran the rest of the way under the cover of the mountain. When they reached the top, Zack and the gang peered out across the temple courtyard. The ginkgo tree shined under the glow of the moon. The ancient tree was absolutely gigantic, with a trunk that was easily the width of a highway. Seven massive limbs branched off the trunk and reached to the sky, holding up what looked like a thick, puffy hairdo of yellow leaves. It was magnificent.

"There it is," Zack whispered excitedly.

"It's beautiful . . . ," Olivia said.

Zack scanned the grounds for danger. The super zombies were nowhere in sight. Just the lone watchman at the top of the steps.

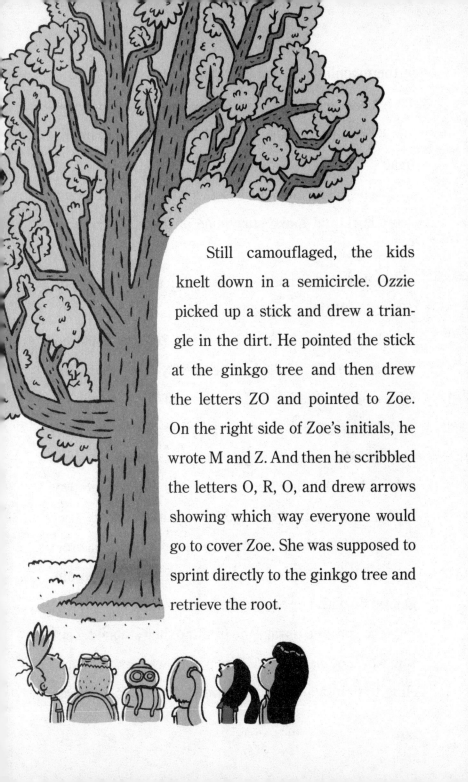

Still camouflaged, the kids knelt down in a semicircle. Ozzie picked up a stick and drew a triangle in the dirt. He pointed the stick at the ginkgo tree and then drew the letters ZO and pointed to Zoe. On the right side of Zoe's initials, he wrote M and Z. And then he scribbled the letters O, R, O, and drew arrows showing which way everyone would go to cover Zoe. She was supposed to sprint directly to the ginkgo tree and retrieve the root.

"Wait a second, I don't get it," Rice whispered. "What are all the letters for? Is that some kind of code?"

"The letters are us, nimrod," Zoe said, shaking her head.

"The plan's simple, Rice," said Zack. "We watch Zoe's back and make sure none of the super zombies gets close to her."

"Oh . . ." Rice nodded. "Why didn't you just say so?"

"Shhh!" they all said in unison.

As they proceeded with the plan, Zoe crept out from the underbrush, flanked on her left by Ozzie, Rice, and Olivia, and on the left by Madison and Zack.

Zack clutched a bo staff in his hands, his eyes searching for kung fu super zombies. Madison walked behind him, holding her rattan sticks. She looked over her shoulder as they crossed into enemy territory. Rice and Ozzie held their nunchaku at the ready. Olivia crept behind them, walking backward, keeping an eye out, geared up with her own rattan sticks.

Zoe sprinted toward the tree and then stopped. Zack saw why Zoe had halted. A trip wire was set up, encircling the ginkgo tree. There were also Spazola Energy

Cola cans, filled with rocks, which hung from wires off the tree—if she hit them, they'd make enough noise to alert the super zombies. It was a trap.

"See?" Rice whispered as Zoe stepped over the primitive alarm system. "They're not that smart."

Now past the trip wire, Zoe climbed over the fence and neared the ancient ginkgo. She stepped around the base of the tree and suddenly a series of thumps shook the ground. The kung fu super zombies appeared out of nowhere, surrounding them. Their heads were shaved, and their scalps were pale white and crinkly, like the rest of their skin. Their eyes were ink black and soulless. They looked like they meant serious business.

"Okay, guys," Ozzie said. "I think it's time for plan B. . . ."

"What's plan B?" Olivia asked.

"Fight!"

In a mad rush forward, Zack and the gang clashed with the super zombies.

Zack twirled his bo and thrust the wooden staff at a zombie's midriff. The super zombie blocked the opening gambit and then hit Zack in the chest with a counterblow that sent Zack flying.

Zack shook off the shock of the hit and looked up. The rest of his friends were fighting fearlessly, using all the moves they had learned over the past few days, but there were too many kung fu super zombies for them to deal with all at once.

"Retreat!" Ozzie shouted as five super zombies came at him together, fighting as one unit.

Zack scrambled up to his feet and tried to run away, but someone tripped him from behind and he fell face forward to the ground. The super zombie pounced on Zack's back as he tried to get away. Zack felt himself getting pulled back at the waist.

He twisted his body as Zhang had taught him and clenched his legs around the zombie's neck, putting it in a headlock with his knees. Zack felt the super zombie lose its grip and twisted his hips in a quick swivel.

The monk spun in the air and landed in a heap. Zack scrambled to his feet, but a searing pain ripped through his waist. Another super zombie had come up from his blind side and bitten down hard on his hip.

A chunk of Zack's skin ripped off in the undead freak's diseased and rotten mouth.

CHAPTER

As the group sprinted away from the temple, Zack hobbled behind. He was trying to keep up, despite the sharp pain shooting down his leg and up his rib cage. He glanced over his shoulder, but he couldn't tell if the monks had given chase. It didn't seem like it. They were smarter than that. They must have been under strict orders not to leave the tree unguarded. But Zack guessed there would still be a few who came after them, once they realized they had just had a brush with Olivia Jenkins, the vital vegan, the zombie antidote.

Zack's limp worsened as he ran down the mountain, and he tripped, collapsing in the dirt. The rest of the group doubled back and gathered around him.

"Come on, little bro," Zoe said. "Get off your butt. . . ."

"ACK!" Zack gasped as he lifted his shirt to check out his wound.

"OMG, Zack, are you okay?" Olivia stopped and crouched down next to him.

"Ooooh," Rice said with horrified fascination. "That looks nasty!"

"It bit me!" was Zack's delayed response. "It took a huge bite out of me!"

"Shhhh!" Ozzie said. "Do you think we lost them?"

"I haven't seen any," Madison said. "I think so. . . ."

Olivia grabbed Zack under his arms. "Help me get him over there."

They dragged Zack off the track and laid him down under a thick cover of leaves. Zoe and Ozzie stood lookout, while Madison, Olivia, and Rice crouched down at Zack's side.

The kung fu super zombie had chomped into Zack's hip, through the fabric of his waistband, and ripped off a huge flap of skin in the process. A dark red stain ran down the side of his pant leg. He didn't want to look at it, but he couldn't tear his eyes away.

Zack could see the white fatty tissue around the rim of the bite wound. He was mesmerized by how deep it was. Pure curiosity overtook him as he stared at his hip. He extended his pinky finger and pressed his fingertip on the exposed bone. Then he poked and prodded at the jagged gash in his side. It stung like nothing he'd ever felt before and the pain made him nauseous.

"Don't do that," Madison said. "You're going to infect it."

Zack thought he was going to puke.

"Zack, man, are you okay?" Rice asked.

"He doesn't look okay," said Olivia.

Zack was not okay. If he still had the ability to speak, he would have told them so, but they would figure it out on their own. Zack listened to his friends. His head felt like a watermelon on a toothpick. His eyes glazed over.

"Is he going to zombify?" Olivia's voice said.

Rice made a skeptical noise. "Zack can't zombify—he's

immune, like the rest of us."

"Yeah, but that was only the regular zombie virus," said Madison. "He just got bitten by a super zombie. . . ."

"What, you think he's going to turn into—"

Zack could feel the turbocharged super zombie mutation shooting through every vein, artery, and capillary, taking over his entire body. He tried to say something, but all that came out was a choked gargling sound. He felt his muscles starting to spasm involuntarily. Zack swallowed and gasped. He couldn't breathe. He was dying.

Or rather undying. Zack knew the feeling. He had been a zombie once before, but this felt different.

The last thing he remembered before giving up on the impulse to breathe were the two super zombies jumping out of the bushes and his friends springing into action. Zack's vision blurred and he could feel his heart skip a beat, each one getting farther apart from the last, until finally his heart stopped altogether. His head lolled to the side as he collapsed in the dirt.

* * *

Zack's eyes flicked open and he could see no color, only black and white. He was still lying down and his hip didn't hurt at all anymore. He sat up slowly, a command that his body did on its own—his mind seemed to have little or no control over his movements. He glanced down at his hands. The skin was already starting to crinkle and whiten. His stomach roared with hunger.

He heard a rustle in the leaves and his neck craned

toward the sound. In his newly color-blind field of vision, five people came into view, dragging two unconscious bodies across the ground.

One of the people turned toward Zack, the plump one with eyeglasses. "Dude!" he called out. "You're alive!" He ran toward Zack, and Zack leaped off the ground, took two running steps forward, and tackled the chubby person to the ground.

"Ahhhhh!" the chunky one yelled. "He's a super zombie! Get him off me!"

Zack gnawed at the air, trying to clamp down and bite into the skull of this shrieking human. All he wanted to do was consume whatever living brains he could. The hunger in his belly demanded it.

"Dude, chill, it's me, Rice!" the chubby one screamed, squirming on his back. "It's me, man! Stop it!"

Suddenly, Zack focused really hard on controlling the unstoppable hunger inside him. He regained control of his motor functions for a moment and looked at the boy whose brains he was about to eat. He saw his best friend underneath him. Disgusted, Zack jumped up to his feet and backed away from him. The rest of the people circled around him—his sister, Zoe; Madison; Ozzie; Olivia—they all stood around, holding their martial arts weapons. Zack felt like a frightened animal, backing away, then lashing out, snarling as they closed in.

"Easy, Zack," Ozzie said, whirling his nunchaku around slowly. "We're your friends. We don't want to hurt you."

"Can you understand what we're saying to you?" Zoe pronounced each syllable very clearly, as if she was talking to a baby.

"Snarl once if you can understand us," Rice said, getting to his feet and brushing the dirt off his pants.

Zack let out one hideous snarl and bared his teeth, hissing.

"Whoa!" Madison said. "Look, he can understand us!"

"That doesn't prove

anything," Zoe said. "He could've just been snarling."

Rice then held up three fingers. "How many fingers am I holding up?"

What—do they think I'm some kind of idiot? Zack thought inside his super zombie brain and then snarled three times.

"See?" Rice said. "He can understand!"

"I think he's trying not to eat us, but it's hard for him," Olivia said. "Poor little guy."

Zack didn't know how long he could keep control of his impulses. It was getting more difficult by the second. The hunger was about to take over when something happened.

Zack's friends' voices faded out and he heard another voice. It was like someone was sending a signal directly to his brain. It was Zhang Wu, uttering his mantra over and over again:

You must BE the zombie. . . . You MUST be the zombie. . . . YOU must be the zombie!

Then Zack's eyes flipped from black and white back to color and everything became clear.

He knew exactly what he had to do.

CHAPTER 16

I must BE the zombie! Zack thought to himself. He breathed in deeply, wheezily, and grunted, flexing all his muscles at once. The hunger still raged in his stomach, but he was certain he could control it, at least for a short while. To do what he needed to do. What the whole world needed him to do.

"Check it out." Rice pointed excitedly at his buddy. "He's not attacking us anymore."

"Don't go near him, Rice," Madison said. "He might be suckering us."

"Yeah, he's smarter than he looks," said Zoe. "Always has been."

"No, I can tell," Rice said. "He's not going to hurt us." Rice stepped closer to his undead friend and stuck his hand out like a stranger saying hello to a dog.

"Rice," Ozzie said in a commanding voice, "please step away from the super Zack!"

But Rice didn't listen. He stuck his hand right in front of Zack's mouth. "See?"

Zack's stomach growled violently. It took every ounce of effort not to sink his teeth into Rice's meaty arm.

"He's not gonna bite us," Rice said. "He knows who we are."

If Rice had any idea how close he was to getting his face ripped off and his brains eaten out of his skull, he would have stood back at least a few feet. Zack had to get out of there quick. He turned his back on his friends and walked away.

"Super Zack, wait!" Olivia called.

"Oh, please don't call him that," Zoe groaned. "It's exactly what he wants you to call him."

"Where are you going?"

Zack grunted and pointed to the base of a nearby tree. "Rrr-oot!" He struggled to say the monosyllabic word. He wasn't even going to try to say *ginkgo*.

"Hold on," Madison said, picking up her kung fu sticks. "We'll come with you, Super Zack!"

"Okay," said Zoe, losing her patience. "The next one of you who calls him that is going to get smacked."

Zack looked at his friends, then shook his head. He turned around, leaving them behind.

"Wait!" Ozzie called after him. He was stripping off the orange robe from the smaller of the two zombies. Ozzie jogged over to Super Zack and handed him the monk attire. Ozzie looked into Zack's eyes. Zack wanted nothing more than to eat his friend's brains, but fought back the urge. Ozzie bowed respectfully and backed away as Zack went off to finish what they had come here to do.

Back atop the mountain, Zack watched from the shadows as the entire super-zombified monastery walked around the ginkgo tree. He put on the orange robe to blend in. Zack walked out into the moonlit courtyard of the temple and lumbered through the crowd. *I must BE the zombie*, Super Zack kept thinking. *I must BE the zombie.* He went around the back of the tree where he would be hidden from view.

Super Zack then reached his hand underneath the base of the tree trunk. He could feel the power of the ancient ginkgo in his hand as he gripped the rough bark. He could feel the super zombie strength in his own arm as well. Zack pulled as hard as he could and broke off a large piece of the root above the surface of the dirt. Quickly, he moved back from the tree.

When he looked up, Super Zack found himself surrounded by two dozen super zombie monks. They glared at him, snarling and flaring their nostrils. The super zombies formed a ring around him and tackled Zack.

Zack forced his mind to go blank.

Time seemed to slow down, like freeze-frames in a movie, as Zack lost control of his body. Zhang's voice filled his mind's ear once again. *You ARE the zombie!*

Zack's arms jabbed and punched with tremendous

speed and power as he peppered the first wave of super zombie attackers with sharp, lightning-quick blows. His legs flung round and kick-flipped over three more super zombies, and he took them down with a single back-heel roundhouse. It was as if he was being controlled remotely by a video gamer, hitting combos for the next move.

When Zack regained control, he was standing in a sea of broken bodies, all lying on the ground.

He couldn't believe that he was still alive. Well, not technically *alive*, but still in one piece.

"Whoa!" Rice shouted, almost laughing at the scene before him. "That was insane, Super Zack!"

Zoe then appeared behind Rice and smacked him in the back of his head. "What did I tell you?"

"Ow!" Rice yelled. "Not cool!"

The rest of them came out from hiding behind the temple—Ozzie, Madison, Olivia, and Twinkles—and looked on, completely in awe of what Super Zack had done.

Zack was exhausted. He felt like he could lie down

and go to sleep for a thousand years. He stumbled toward his friends and dropped to his knees, letting the ginkgo root fall to the ground.

The hunger was back, and worse than ever. He wanted to eat brains very badly. Zack lunged at Ozzie when he bent down to pick up the root.

"Braaiiins!" Zack cried, clawing at his friend. Ozzie snatched up the root and jumped back.

"Easy, boy!" Rice shouted, pulling out a bottle of ginkgo biloba pills that he still had in his backpack. Madison, Zoe, and Olivia held Zack by the wrists and ankles. Rice stood over him and opened the bottle, pouring the ginkgo pellets into his mouth. Ozzie put Zack in a headlock and forced his mouth closed until he swallowed them all.

As he faded out of consciousness, he could feel his friends hoist him up and start to carry him down the mountainside. He heard Olivia say, "Let's get out of here before those kung fu freakazoids wake up."

CHAPTER

Zack woke up to his friends standing over him, their eyes gazing down at him. They were back in Zhang's hut. Zack lay flat on his back on the bottom bunk. His hands and feet were tied to the bedposts. Zhang undid the rope and Zack sat up.

"What's going on?" Zack asked. "I just had the weirdest dream. . . . I dreamed I was a super zombie."

"Dude," said Rice, "you were. You don't remember?"

"From what I hear, you handled yourself like a true master." Zhang gave Zack a knowing wink and smiled.

Zack blinked as he wrapped his head around what they were telling him. "So . . . I was really a super

zombie?" he said. "But I'm not now. . . ."

Madison explained. "We mixed the mayfly larvae with the piece of the ginkgo root you got. Then we added some of the frilled shark enzyme and some of Olivia's blood. Then we just dropped a little in your mouth and voila!"

"No more Super Zack," Zoe said, and made a little celebratory woo-hoo sound.

"The antidote worked, Zack!" Olivia said, holding a piece of gauze over the spot on her arm where they had taken her blood sample. "Now we can get the ingredients back to Nigel so he can figure out a way to mass-produce it and save my brother and my mom and my dad and everyone else!"

Zack could hardly believe it, yet he knew it was true. The whole episode seemed like a bad dream he could barely remember. He looked up at Zhang. "I'm sorry I doubted you," Zack told him.

"You have nothing to apologize for," Zhang said. "You were ready when it counted most."

Ozzie walked up to Zhang. "Well, I have something to apologize for. I'm sorry for the way I acted when we first met. . . ."

Zhang brushed off the apology with a swipe of his hand. "You are young and brash, but you are very skilled. You have proven yourself worthy and then some."

"Okay, can we please cool it with all this mushy stuff," Zoe said, cupping her ear as if she was listening to something far off in the distance. "You guys hear that?"

They all stopped and listened. Zack could hear the yowls of the remaining super zombies echo down from the mountaintop. The noise made him shudder.

Zhang's expression changed back to the serious look they knew so well. "We must go," he said. "Quickly! Follow me!"

The seven of them rushed outside and Zhang led them to a small garage. Twinkles tagged along. Zhang opened the door to the garage and hopped in the front seat of an old beat-up pickup truck. "Get in!" he shouted, and the kids jumped into the truck bed. "Hang on!" Zhang hollered as he floored the gas pedal and peeled out down the narrow dirt road.

They arrived at the Hangzhou airport a short while later, and Zhang pulled onto the runway. Zack could see their plane not far ahead.

They were in the clear.

But as they drove across the tarmac, a large mob emerged, forming a super zombie army between them and their plane.

"Oh, now what the heck is this?" Zack said in the front seat.

"There's no way we can get past that many with just the seven of us . . . ," Ozzie said from the back of the pickup.

"You're right," Zhang said, slowing down the truck. "Zack, take the wheel. I know what I must do."

Zack shot the kung fu master a look of confusion.

Zhang pointed at the horde of super zombies and said very calmly, "Drive straight at them. I will hold them off."

Zack hesitated for a moment.

"Hold on, Zhang," Zoe said, sticking her head in from the back. "What's the plan here?"

"I will keep them occupied while you get to your airplane," Zhang said. "It's the only way. There are too many of them."

"But they'll rip you apart," Zack said. "Even you, Zhang."

"I'll be fine, young Zachary. I am a kung fu master!"

"I'm not doing that," Zack said. "We're not leaving you behind!"

"There's no destiny but the one before us," said Zhang. He revved the engine and took a long, deep breath. He floored the accelerator, putting the pedal to the metal, and zoomed straight for the gigantic swarm.

As they sped across the tarmac, Zhang opened the driver's-side door and shouted. "Take the wheel!"

Zack had no other choice. He leaned over from the passenger seat and grabbed the steering wheel.

Zhang Wu leaped out of the moving vehicle and kicked the door shut with one fluid motion.

Outside, he landed in front of the super zombie crowd, one man against a thousand howling, snarling zombie mutants.

Zack quickly scooted over into the driver's seat and pressed his foot on the accelerator, plowing through the undead horde where Zhang had cleared them a path.

Zack glanced back in the rearview mirror and watched the old kung fu master take them on. Zack was surprised to see that Zhang was winning. The old man was amazing as he defeated one zombie after another.

Zack slammed to a halt beside their jet. They all jumped out of the pickup and scurried up the ramp to board the plane. Madison checked the plane for any super zombie stowaways while Ozzie prepared the jet for liftoff. Less than a minute later, Ozzie wheeled the plane around, pointing it down the runway. The engine rumbled to life, and the jet rolled forward, picking up speed and soaring into the air.

As they cruised high in the sky Zack could see that Zhang was still fighting off the super zombies on the tarmac. Zack reminded himself to never mess with the old kung fu master—ever. *Get out of there, man,* Zack thought to himself. *Get out of there.*

And then Zack heard the voice inside his head.

Young Zack . . . It was Zhang. *I have fulfilled my destiny. And now you and your friends must fulfill yours.*

Against all odds, they had collected the three ingredients they needed—the digestive enzyme from the giant frilled tiger shark, the mayfly larvae from Madagascar, and the root from the ancient ginkgo.

And now they had their cure.

Once they got the samples back to Nigel Black, the super zombies were about to find out what Zack and his friends were really made of.

Hopefully it was more than flesh and brains.

CHAPTER 18

ack on Nigel's private island fortress, the six of them walked from the beach into the rocky cave. The place seemed still and quiet. They walked up to the steel door leading to the research lab. Zack punched in the pass code for the door lock Nigel had given them. Slowly they entered the zombie-proof compound with extreme caution.

"Hello?" Zack called out, his voice echoing down the hallway. "Nigel! Anybody home?"

"We're back!" Zoe chimed in, but there wasn't a peep. The whole place was eerily quiet.

"Let's go check the main lab," Rice said, leading the

way. "He's probably in there."

The double doors swung open as they pushed into Nigel's laboratory. They were expecting to see Cousin Ben strapped to the table, still super-zombified. But there was no one there. Instead, the place was a complete mess. The examination table, where Ben had been, was flipped over on its side. The computer equipment, the stainless steel lab tools, the glass flasks and beakers were all scattered and smashed on the floor.

Thick red streaks of blood zigzagged, smeared across the linoleum tiles.

It looked like a crime scene.

"What the heck happened here?" Ozzie asked.

"I was thinking the same thing," Zack said.

"Something not good," Madison said, raising her eyebrows. "Obvi."

As they scanned the wreckage, looking for any more clues, the double doors suddenly locked behind them.

WHAM! CLACK! Something grumbled in the hallway.

Rice spun on his heels. "Whoa, what was that?"

"Again probably something not good," Madison repeated. "When are you guys gonna learn?"

Zack raced toward the door. He pulled at the handle, but the door was bolted shut. He stood on his tiptoes and peered through the small square window at the top of the door.

He gasped at the scene, and his stomach twisted into a tight, painful knot.

In the harsh fluorescent light of hallway, Ben lifted

his shriveled arm. Another super zombie high-fived Olivia's brother. That super zombie was *Nigel Black.* His face wrinkled up into a sinister scowl. His eyes were bloodshot and red. Thick veins bulged off his forehead, pulsing with the super zombie virus.

"Bad news, guys," Zack hollered to his friends. "Nigel's a freakin' super zombie!"

"We got a visual?" asked Ozzie.

"I did," Zack said. "But I lost them. They ran down the hallway."

"Why'd they do that?" Zoe asked. "Olivia's in here!"

"I don't know why," Zack shouted. "I'm not a super zombie anymore!"

It suddenly dawned on him. Zack was the only person in the entire world who had been un-super-zombified.

Now the super zombies had them trapped.

"What are we going to do now?" Zoe asked.

"I don't know about you guys," Rice said, "but I'm gonna mix up more of the antidote." He dumped the contents of his backpack onto a metal counter and set out the three ingredients for the super zombie cure: the digestive enzyme from the giant frilled tiger shark. Check. Unhatched larvae from the African mayfly of Madagascar. Check. The root from the ancient ginkgo tree. Check.

Zack called to his buddy on the other side of the lab. "Rice, get crackin'."

He continued to keep watch while Rice directed Zoe, Madison, and Ozzie on how to help him mix up a batch of the antidote. Then the hallway's fluorescent lights flickered and went dead. Zack couldn't see a thing.

"Hurry up, guys, I think they're coming back!"

"You think?" Madison said.

"I don't know—they shut off the lights in the

hallway," said Zack, squinting through the window.

Madison scooped up an unbroken beaker. Zoe found a stirring stick and Ozzie grabbed an empty plastic spray bottle. They ran over and gave the items to Rice, who was waiting impatiently with the super-antidote ingredients.

"Chop-chop!" Rice said, clapping his hands together. "Let's get it together, people. . . . Olivia, we're going to need just a little bit more of your blood."

Olivia went over to the lab counter as Rice dumped a bottle of Vital Vegan PowerPunch into the beaker. He then added three small portions of the ingredients and stirred them up.

Ozzie pulled out a sharp metal pin and gestured for Olivia to hold out her finger. He cleaned it with an alcohol wipe, then raised the pin above her fingertip. Olivia looked away.

"Wait, Olivia," said Ozzie. "You don't have to do this. You're going to pass out and those super zombies could come in here any second."

"That's a good point, cuz," Madison said. "You pass out anytime someone takes your blood. You were out for ten whole minutes in China."

"But we need her to do it one more time," Rice said.

"I hate to say it, but Rice is right, guys," Olivia said. "The only way to stop all this craziness is if we make as much of the antidote as we can."

Olivia held out her finger and winced as Ozzie pricked her skin with the needle. He held out a test tube and caught the red droplets before Olivia swooned and dropped to the floor.

WHOMP! BAM!

Zack stumbled back as the double doors flew open. Ben and Nigel lumbered in, side by side, and a rotten stench filled the air. The two super zombies staggered to a stop, their chests heaving in and out, *wheeze-grunt, wheeze-grunt, wheeze.*

"Told ya we shouldn't have let her give the blood!" Madison said.

"No time for I told you so's," Zack yelled. "Rice, how's that antidote coming along?"

Rice was tapping a drop of Olivia's blood into the mixture and swirling it around in the glass beaker. "Almost ready, Zackarino!"

"Growr!" said Nigel Black as he lurched forward. He had a nasty bite mark on his arm that was red and green and black from blood and pus and zombie rot. Ben split off from his partner and tottered to the right. Both super zombies eyed the group, like predators about to lunge for their prey.

"Everybody, form a circle around Olivia!" Ozzie shouted, and hopped over Olivia's body. Zack backed up, putting himself between the super zombies and their friend. The girls did the same.

As the two super zombies zeroed in, Rice finished

mixing the solution and began pouring the pink liquid into the spray bottle.

"Glarghk!" Nigel Black made the first move, shouldering past Zoe and leaping for Rice.

"Rice, look out!" Zack cried.

"Whoa!" Rice looked up to see Nigel diving to tackle him.

Nigel Black slammed into Rice just as he twisted the spray nozzle closed. The two of them crashed to the floor.

The rest of the antidote wobbled and tipped off the side of the table. Zack dashed for the falling container, stretching his arms out like a football player. He felt the glass in his hands as he skidded across the floor. *Phew*, he'd saved the super zombie antidote.

Olivia was still passed out in the middle of the room. Cousin Ben charged and clashed with Ozzie, Madison, and Zoe. In the other direction, Rice was wrestling on the floor with Nigel Black. The super zombie clawed on top of Rice, straddling him. He knocked the antidote out of Rice's hands and the plastic bottle slid across the floor.

Rice scrambled, reaching for the spray bottle. Zack set the beaker back on the counter and bolted for the antidote. He grabbed the bottle off the floor and curled his finger around the plastic trigger. He aimed it right at Nigel's super-zombified face and squeezed.

The pink liquid spritzed the super zombie in the eyes and the mouth.

Nigel Black hacked and coughed as the antidote absorbed into his system.

The super zombie dropped in a heap on top of Rice, who breathed a sigh of relief.

"Rooowrghghkle!"

Before Zack could help Rice to his feet, Cousin Ben gave a phlegm-rattling roar. Ozzie and the girls were all over him. Ozzie hugged him around the waist, Madison clung tightly to one of her cousin's arms, and Zoe was on the floor, with both hands wrapped around his leg, trying to pull him down.

"Hang on tight!" Ozzie groaned.

"He's too strong!" Madison shouted.

In three quick movements, Ben erupted in a burst of super zombie energy. He kicked his leg and sent Zoe sliding across the floor, crashing into a shelf. The super zombie whipped his arm to the side and flung Madison into the opposite wall. Ben wiggled his hips like he was doing the hula and Ozzie flew into the overturned gurney. Ozzie tried to get up, but he looked woozy from the fall and collapsed on his side.

Ben beat his chest, picked up his sister, Olivia, and flopped her over his shoulder. In a flash, he made a break for the laboratory door, stealing away with the last known source of the vital vegan antidote.

"Olivia!" Zack sprang to his feet and ran after Ben. "Olivia!"

Slung over her brother's shoulder, Olivia's eyes twitched open and she came to. "Ahhh! Zack! Help!" She squirmed to get away, but Ben carried his sister as easily as if she was a rag doll.

The super zombie lumbered around the corner at the end of the dark hallway, making his way back toward the sea cave. Zack was trying to catch up, but the super zombie was way ahead of him.

Zack burst outside and the salty air blasted him in the face.

VRRRRooooMM!

Zack shaded his eyes and peered out at the open

sea. Cousin Ben was steering a speedboat. Olivia was tied up in the back of the boat, kicking and screaming as they zoomed out onto the water.

Then they were gone.

Zack's mind reeled. There were no other boats in sight. A tight panic set into his chest and his heart sank to the pit of his stomach. He stood there helplessly, then kicked the sand and said a word that his mother would have sent him to his room for saying.

Without a second more to waste, Zack doubled back to the laboratory to see if Nigel could remember any-thing from his super-zombification.

Back in Nigel's lab, the rest of the gang were picking themselves up off the floor.

"Where's Olivia?" Madison asked as he walked in.

"Cousin Ben's got her," Zack said.

His friends' faces fell all at once.

"I think he's taking her back to Florida—you know, back to their parents so they can use her to make more brains for all the other super zombies. That was their original plan. . . ."

"Then, what are we waiting for?" Madison shouted. "Let's get out of here and go save my cousin!"

"Not so fast," Nigel groaned from the floor, raising his arm up to stop them. "We have to make some preparations first. . . ."

The six of them gathered around Nigel, who was unable to stand on his own.

Twinkles trotted up to Nigel and licked him on the nose while Madison and Ozzie knelt down beside him and helped him sit up.

"Are you all right, man?" Rice asked him.

Nigel shook his head. "No, I think I'm pretty far from all right," he said.

"At least you're not super-zombified anymore," Zoe said. "Show a little gratitude."

"Come on." Nigel rose to his feet and began picking up the pieces of his lab. "We haven't much time."

The Florida heat was thick and sticky.

Zack was crawling on his belly, flat to the ground, the way soldiers do in combat. He was alone. Nigel Black and the rest of the crew were spread out around the epicenter of super zombies. The zombies surrounded Bunco's bubblegum factory, where this whole super zombie fiasco had begun a little over a week ago.

Ozzie had flown them in Nigel's small propeller plane while they scoped out the scene below. The super zombies were all crowding together like they were at an outdoor rock concert. And Olivia was the headlining act. There were probably about two or three hundred of the brain-hungry suckers.

Led by Uncle Conrad and Aunt Ginny, the super

zombies had rounded up a whole bunch of regular zombies. One by one, the super zombies were going to unzombify the regulars, turning them back into humans so they could feast on their brains.

It was going to be super gross.

That was unless Zack Clarke had anything to say about it. He crawled on his elbows, clutching a green Super Soaker filled with the antidote. He had an extra container full of antidote for refills. Two spray bottles were holstered on each hip. He also had a backpack filled with antidote water balloons. They sloshed as he walked toward the zombies.

Everyone else had about the same amount of anti-dote. They'd mixed up as big a batch as they could, using a case of the vegan vitamin water Nigel had in storage,

the rest of Olivia's blood sample, and the special ingredients they had gathered from across the globe.

Zack checked the stopwatch that he had synced with the rest of his friends. Thirty seconds remained. He saw Rice about forty yards away. His buddy glanced his way and gave him the thumbs-up. They hid just outside the perimeter, behind parked cars and the bushes lining the factory grounds. Inching forward, they were finally close enough to run into the crowd.

The stopwatch beeped and Zack silenced it. He quietly sprinted forward, his squirt gun poised.

Ready.

All seven of them appeared, encircling the undead horde. Twinkles was literally armed to the teeth, carrying a small antidote-filled water balloon in his mouth.

Aim.

This better work, he thought. And he knew it would. As long as they

all fought together. Zack ran up behind the super zombie horde, ready to end this once and for all.

Fire.

A dozen red and green water balloons sailed through the air, headed straight for the swarm of brain eaters.

A Few Months Later...

Zack sat on the couch in Madison Miller's living room.

Next to him, Rice had a plate piled high with cheese, crackers, and salami balancing on his lap.

"Great party, Madison," Rice said, chewing with his mouth open. "Good snacks."

"Thanks, Rice," she said. "Glad you're having a good time."

Zack glanced out the window into the backyard. There must have been fifty people all milling around, former zombies, former super zombies. Zack's mom and dad were talking to R. J. Bunco, the owner of the Fun World amusement park. Rice's parents were chatting it up with Thaddeus Duplessis, the creator of BurgerDog, who was at the grill, cooking hot dogs and hamburgers for everyone. Zack watched as Madison's dad tapped Duplessis on the shoulder and swiped the spatula and tongs away from the mad scientist who had started the whole zombie outbreak in the first place.

Twinkles was by the grill, too, and eating a hamburger patty that had fallen in the grass.

At least there won't be any burgers that taste like a dog at this barbecue, Zack thought with a chuckle. *Only a dog tasting a burger.*

 Zhang Wu couldn't make the trip. Zack and the gang had received word that the kung fu master had made it out alive. However, he was still in China recovering from his battle with the super zombies. But at least Nigel was there, along with Ozzie and his dad, General Briggs. Greg Bansal-Jones was holding a tray full of appetizers and passing them around to the crowd. Zoe was by his side, flirting with him a little. Nadie and her parents had even been able to make it, and she had a lemur sitting on her shoulder.

Uncle Conrad and Aunt Ginny were eating hamburgers with Ben and Olivia. Everyone was like a big happy family again.

For the most part.

They had some battle scars. And some missing fingers. And even a couple of missing arms and legs. But all in all, they were all just fine and dandy once again. Just everyone hanging out for a late summer barbecue.

Rice nudged Zack in the ribs.

"Huh?" Zack asked, stealing a cracker from Rice's plate.

"We're about to be on TV, man. How cool is that?"

"Pretty cool, dude," Zack said. "Pretty cool."

"I just hope they get the part right where I saved the world from super zombies almost single-handedly. . . ."

Zack glared at his friend and crinkled his brow. "You did what?"

"Just kidding." Rice laughed. "Just seeing if you were paying attention." He chewed another bite of pepperoni. "Did you see Mandy Pitman's here?"

"Oh yeah?" said Zack.

"I heard she likes you," Rice said.

"Okay, whatever . . ."

"I bet she'd let you take her to the dance next week," said Rice.

"I hate dances," Zack said.

"Just saying," Rice said. "I heard she likes you."

"I heard that, too, Zack," Madison said innocently before getting up from the sofa. She stuck her head out the patio door and called out to the people in the back-yard. "The show's about to start!"

They all gathered inside and piled in the living room with plates of hot dogs and hamburgers. Madison's mom turned up the television volume.

A special edition of *Nigel Black's Unnatural Wonders: The Zombie Chasers* was about to begin.

Nigel's voice opened over a shot of Zack's street: "It was the best of days; it was the worst of days when Zack Clarke came home one Friday night to find his sister, Zoe, and her best friends having a sleepover. Little did he know—"

Zoe interrupted: "that he was going to get punked like no one has ever been punked before."

"Shhhhh, Zoe." Zack elbowed his sis.

"You shhhhh, twerp!" She elbowed him back.

"I told you first."

"I told you second."

"Will both of you shush up?" Rice said. "My part's coming up!"

"You mean the part where you messed everything

up and created super smart zombies that almost killed us all?" Zoe asked.

Rice raised his eyebrows. "Among others. . . . Besides, how many times did I save your butt?"

"Please," she said. "You're the one who needed all the butt saving."

"Hey, guys," Olivia said. "Stop talking about everyone's butts. There are people trying to eat here."

It was good to get back to normal, Zack thought.

At least for the time being.

But Zack had a feeling that nothing was going to be completely normal ever again.

And that was okay with him.

Normal was overrated.

Zack smiled and crossed his arms as he watched their tale unfold on TV. How they had met Nigel Black and tracked down the giant frilled tiger shark. How they had flown to Madagascar and then to China in search of the mayfly larvae and the ancient ginkgo tree root to complete the super zombie antidote. How they had ambushed the super zombies in Florida with their antidote-filled Super Soakers and water balloons and saved Olivia Jenkins. And then how they had traveled back to

BurgerDog headquarters, unzombified Duplessis, and remade the popcorn antidote that had reversed the first outbreak. How they had unzombified their families and the air force pilots back in Phoenix. And how they had spent weeks unzombifying the undead masses across the globe. How they had battled the rest of the super zombies and reversed the outbreak completely. How they were heroes who would be remembered forever.

Halfway through the show, Rice turned to Zack and whispered in his ear.

"You know what's superduper cool?"

"No, Rice," Zack said. "Tell me."

"When we're back at school, sitting in our history class, we're gonna be studying ourselves!"

Pretty cool, Zack thought. *Pretty cool indeed.*

The satellite dish tilted upward, aiming itself at the night sky. Kevin gave the thumbs-up and TJ hit the send button. Kevin felt his stomach clench as the laser refracted through the prism, shot out through the satellite dish, and carried their message to the universe across the black, starry night.

"So what happens now?" Kevin asked.

"We wait for the aliens," said Warner. "Obviously."

Kevin settled cross-legged into the grass and started to jot down the sequence of events in his log.

11:30 p.m.: No response yet.

11:37 p.m.: Tara challenges Warner and TJ to a staring contest. Warner blinks first. TJ wins.

11:38 p.m.: Warner challenges Tara to a laughing contest because that's what he thought they were doing in the first place. Tara laughs first.

11:45 p.m.: My butt is getting wet from the wet grass. Should have brought a towel.

11:50 p.m.: Everybody cranky. Warner regrets not bringing snacks. We all regret the no snack bringing, too.

12:00 a.m.: Galactascope still silent.

As Kevin marked the mission failure into his log, he felt his stomach tighten with panic. Even if there were aliens out there, it could take months for them to get the message, and they only had a few days before the convention.

"Come on, guys," Kevin said, his face crestfallen. "Let's pack up and get out of here before we get in trouble. We can try again tomorrow."

"Are you sure you don't want to wait a little longer, Kev?" Tara asked. "I could stay up a little laaaaaay-ter." She yawned, stretching her arms out.

THUNK! Tara's wrist whacked the device, and the galactascope abruptly began to blip and bleep. The laptop monitor flashed to life, and a long, repetitive jumble of ones and zeroes appeared on the screen.

"What'd you do?" Warner asked.

"I didn't mean to!" Tara scowled at Warner then looked at the computer. "What the heck is that?"

"It's a message," Kevin whispered, his voice tinged with anticipation.

They watched as the coded message scrolled down the computer screen, stopping abruptly and morphing into English through a neat little translator programming code that TJ had installed. "SOS. Need interstellar coordinates. SOS. Need interstellar coordinates. SOS."

"Quick," Warner said. "Send it a map of our solar system."

TJ typed frantically on the laptop, pulling up a diagram of Earth's solar system.

"Now give it our longitude and latitude," said Kevin.

They waited in suspense by the lakeside, hoping for a reply. "I don't know," Kevin said, beginning to get discouraged after ten minutes of silence. "Maybe someone's messing with us?"

"But no one knows we're even out here," Warner said.

Alexander, Kevin thought. *Is he spying on us?*

"Come on, Kevin," said Tara. "It has to be real. Let's try it again." She turned to TJ. "Resend the coordinates, Teej."

TJ nodded, interlocking his fingers and pushing out the palms of his hands. As his knuckles cracked, the night sky suddenly opened up with a bright neon-blue flash.

"Whoa," Warner and Tara said together.

Kevin blinked twice, completely speechless. He squinted and watched as a speck of otherworldly light started to grow against the dark backdrop of the sky. At first it looked like a normal star, but as the speck became larger and larger, Kevin could see a UFO hurtling toward them on a billowing trail of gray smoke. *This can't really be happening.*

"Get down!" Kevin shouted as the UFO flew right over their heads.

The four of them ducked for cover as the spacecraft crashed into the lake, sending a large wave rippling toward the shore.

"Holy Moley Mother of Cannoli!" TJ spoke for the first time since the beginning of camp. "Did you just see that?"

Tara, Warner, and Kevin all turned their heads to TJ.

"Dude," Warner said. "I totally forgot you even knew how to talk."

Kevin swiveled his head back and forth, waiting for one of their counselors to check out the commotion, but the camp was still.

"Omigosh," Tara cried out, pointing toward the center of the lake. Something had burst to the surface and was flailing frantically in the water.

"It can't swim," Kevin shouted, and ran toward the paddleboats that were beached on the lakeshore. "We gotta save it! Come on!"

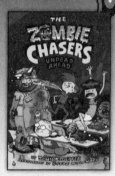

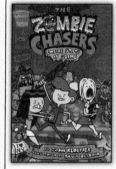

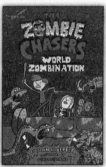